GOD DENIED
A NOVEL

Also by Ellenmorris Tiegerman, PhD
Past Lives Denied: A Novel

GOD DENIED

A NOVEL

Ellenmorris Tiegerman, PhD

© 2025, Ellenmorris Tiegerman. All rights reserved.
Published by Scholar Dreams Publishing, Roslyn, New York
ellenmorrisauthor.com

God Denied: A Novel

ISBN 979-8-9899071-3-7 (paperback)
ISBN 979-8-9899071-2-0 (eBook)

Without limiting the rights under copyright reserved above, no part of this publication may be reproduced, stored in or introduced into a retrieval system, or transmitted in any form or by any means (electronic, mechanical, photocopying, recording, or otherwise, whether now or hereafter known) without the prior written permission of both the copyright owner and the above publisher of this book, except by a reviewer who wishes to quote brief passages in connection with a review written for insertion in a magazine, newspaper, broadcast, website, blog, or other outlet in conformity with United States and International Fair Use or comparable guidelines to such copyright exceptions.

This is a work of the imagination in its entirety. All names, settings, incidents, and dialogue have been invented, and when real places, products, and public figures are mentioned in the story, they are used fictionally and without any claim of endorsement or affiliation. Any resemblance between the characters in the novel and real people is strictly a coincidence.

Publication managed by AuthorImprints.com

Soul recognition may be subtle and slow. A dawning of awareness as the veil is gently lifted. Not everyone is ready to see right away. There is a timing at work, and patience may be necessary for the one who sees first.

—Brian Weiss

TABLE OF CONTENTS

Preface..ix
Author's Note...xi
Prologue: After *Past Lives Denied* 1

1 Will the Real Ashford Connor Stand Up?...............3
2 Campus Life 14
3 Campus Politics 25
4 The Chocolate Chip Committee 37
5 Out of the Frying Pan 49
6 Inching Darkly into the Past..............................58
7 Robertson Redux..63
8 Ash and the Tribe of Judah................................72
9 The Navi Scharf Seminar...................................82
10 The Markowitz Letter.......................................93
11 Game Plan Rising...105
12 The Coalition for Campus Justice....................114
13 The Other Meeting...126
14 The Chocolate Chip Committee Redux 131
15 Buried Truths, Open Wounds........................144
16 The Rebecca Mystery......................................157
17 Impossibly Possible..167

18	Upping the Ante	178
19	The Soul Circle	187
20	Shoes Dropping	201
21	A Call to Purpose	209
22	(Re)birth	217

Acknowledgments 227
About the Author 231

PREFACE

I have worked side by side with my friend and colleague Dr. Ellenmorris Tiegerman for over thirty years. Together we have weathered many storms, first at a university as educators and later at the Tiegerman Schools, which she founded. She has never failed to amaze me, not only with her brilliant mind but also with her openness to new ideas and her ability to implement them with uncommon creativity.

Most people born and raised in the United States treat the idea of past lives and reincarnation with a skeptical eye. It can strike many of us as too ephemeral. Our educational system reinforces that frame of mind. It trains us to accept and think in tangible facts and the inferences they produce, forging a narrow, linear road to understanding of who and why we are and how to make sense of the universe we occupy. Mainstream religions have a major say in this as well. They speak of a solo corporeal life that ends in a final accounting. And even those who do not embrace institutional religion tend to assume we get but a single bite at the apple.

But that is not the case in many other countries. Take India, the second-most-populated country in the world, for example, where reincarnation is embraced as an inseparable part of life's continuous journey. What seems ludicrous or impossible in the West is a cornerstone of belief for countless others elsewhere.

I understand the reluctance to accept the notion of past lives. I, too, was a skeptic. My mind was jammed shut, and it took some coaxing and courage to even consider the possibility that we might have existed in another time and, even more titillating, might occupy more bodies in the future. After I reviewed literature on the topic and began to reassess my life experiences and how I respond in the world, that airtight vault of a mind flew wide open.

Using a multitude of unexplained phenomena of memories of previous lives, Dr. Tiegerman in *God Denied* has created believable characters that we each can relate to and understand. She deftly places them in familiar campus settings and in the greater global community amid the heat and passion of current political and ethnic controversy. She pushes us to think critically, to embrace a wider perspective, and to appreciate the power of eternal connection. What is truth? What is fiction? You decide.

This work and its predecessor, *Past Lives Denied*, have opened my mind to see how our lives are connected in ways I never considered before. Perhaps these spiritual and emotional connective threads can traverse the boundaries of one life and one death and redefine how we see each other and ourselves.

Christine Radziewicz, Doctor of Arts
COO, Tiegerman Schools

AUTHOR'S NOTE

I am mindful that accepting some form of God in our complex lives, let alone the possibility of past lives, does not come easy. It challenges many of us. The concept of past lives verges on the extraordinary and the surreal, making it easy to scoff at the idea. It is my hope, however, that the medium of fiction can incite readers to entertain, ponder, and embrace a different perspective outside the mainstream of modern thinking.

God Denied weaves the religion of politics with the politics of religion, and in that way, seeks to arouse a full range of human senses through which we can explore what in the world we occupy is real, what is our imagination, and what is necessary for our spiritual survival. The narrative that follows invites readers to critically assess and test habitual boundaries, delve into the fantastic, and maybe see what they might otherwise dismiss out of hand.

The political and religious settings, newsworthy events, and God-centric themes will be familiar to readers. What is different, what is less apparent to the raw eye, is what defines and drives those settings. Coincidences? Or some greater force and power that serves as a magnet of connection? My view, as can be imagined, is that we are all here for a purpose that defines our central life mission in the time and place in which we find ourselves.

Past-life regression provides one pathway to personal enlightenment and self-understanding. The central characters in our lives are not accidents. Our soulmates and family and friends, even those whose intersections with us are fleeting, cross our paths for a reason.

The main character in this Book 2 of a trilogy, Ashford Connor, denies the existence of God in his work, his relationships, and his soul. His world is empirically based. Like he did in Book 1, *Past Lives Denied*, he continues to ridicule the notion that a higher power exists that connects us over generations. He is about to have an awakening that leads him on a journey to self-awareness and acceptance. It is a journey available to each of us.

Ellenmorris Tiegerman, PhD

PROLOGUE
AFTER *PAST LIVES DENIED*

After the idiosyncratic Inspector Cormac Robertson, through his deft use of hypnosis and past-life regression, solved the murder of the President of Coronado University and foiled a conspiracy to upend the national educational system, everyone assumed that Professor Caitlyn Morrys, the heroine of *Past Lives Denied*, would become the school president and restore a robust educational culture that prized free speech, scholarship, and the power of learning. But once the dust had settled on the horrific experiences that had occurred on campus, including a bold attempt to make her a second murder victim to avenge a past-life relationship, Caitlyn wanted no part in institutional leadership and politics. She favored a more conventional existence, rebooting her core passion to teach and, not incidentally, to raise a family. She figured she had earned that much.

Her rambunctious partner, Professor Ashford Connor, was more than willing to oblige her. He proposed marriage and she accepted. He also took over her role as chair of the University Personnel Committee and led the way in the quest to deliver to students the talented educators they deserved. When it came to education, he and Caitlyn did not agree on everything, but they shared a strong view that tenure should be the backbone of a sound university educational system, casting aside caprice and politics.

But was that idealistic, even naïve?

Little did Professor Connor know that international events would run roughshod over his plans in a way he could not have anticipated or, for that matter, imagined. The burning question for him would become: Could he move beyond his entrenched views about fate and science and harness the power of past-life regression to solve the challenges that awaited him?

For his part, Inspector Robertson retired from law enforcement, a decision that effectively ended the pursuit of one of the suspects in the gruesome murder of President Uzinski—former Provost Timur Moisescu, who had fled the country. When Professor Morrys asked Robertson about the danger a free Moisescu presented, Robertson assured her that Moisescu had all but certainly changed his identity and relocated to some obscure place in Europe, never to be heard from again. As he told her: "He is no longer a threat to anyone at Coronado University."

1

WILL THE REAL ASHFORD CONNOR STAND UP?

The nightmare erupted without an inkling that anything so disturbing might be lurking.

Where had it come from? Life was grand. Ashford Connor had recently married, and he adored his wife beyond words. He couldn't be happier being with her. The classes he taught filled him with joy, and the feedback he regularly received from students never wavered from excellent. His ascension to chair of the influential and prestigious University Personnel Committee, which handled tenure applications, fulfilled his ever-burning philosophical and political needs. And by all measures, the school's current administration held him in high regard, in spite of his eccentricity and sometimes bombastic—he would say "passionate"—and sarcastic—he would say "keeping everyone honest"—nature.

From his perspective, and certainly that of anyone in close proximity, Ash led an enviable existence. He was living the dream, even better than a dream. The larger community at Coronado University exalted Ashford Connor and Caitlyn Morrys as the campus power couple. Ash had distinguished himself as the most popular teacher and Caitlyn as the most coveted academic advisor. She was gorgeous and athletic; he, handsome out of central casting. They fed off each other, their dialogues like sharply-scripted stage performances featuring contrasting personalities and temperaments. He prided himself on a dry, scathing sense of humor; she wore a perpetual look of earnestness. His words often were razor sharp and unapologetic; she nurtured and affirmed. He exhibited little patience. She listened with a genuinely curious ear. They were worth the price of admission, the unstated envy of school staff and professionals.

Ash had pursued Caitlyn for years but had never been able to demonstrate a long-term commitment, a failing that hovered over their relationship as a potential deal-breaker, as Caitlyn was all about permanence. Their romance underwent habitual roller-coaster swings, passionate and tempestuous until gravity pulled them low. Sometimes when on the high side of the ride, Caitlyn could see the two of them as soulmates "consuming" each other, but whenever the relationship slid downward, the child in Ash moaned that Caitlyn was "too damned intense for normal humankind."

For years, Ash had assumed an imitation of Hugh Grant's petulant and distant character in *Four Weddings and a Funeral*. But serious talk of raising a family had eventually grounded them, and everything between them had changed. Ash seemed to adjust—or "evolve," as Caitlyn said—unearthing that part of him that was a loving, supportive, and attentive partner.

Career-wise, Caitlyn had drifted or, more fairly stated, found her level, like water tends to do. She loved what she did at Coronado University, especially the student-advisory work, which filled her with gratification and a powerful sense of purpose. She received each student with open arms and empathy and selfless commitment. Most needed a sympathetic ear, but others a strong, level voice to offer guidance and advice. Caitlyn held unconventional "unofficial advisement" hours, which suited students fine. They visited on semiprofessional pretexts, carving out time from their otherwise hectic college schedules to talk with her, eagerly waiting in line with fellow students who wore the same hungry looks. Some managed to cajole Caitlyn into seeing them at the house, which did not always sit well with Ash: "Boundaries, Caitlyn, we need some boundaries."

But beyond that, Caitlyn had given up any further ambitions. Her husband, on the other hand, was only getting started. He might not admit it, but he had his sights on greater institutional power, perhaps school president one day. Center stage suited him.

Against that backdrop landed the nightmare. It was an unexpected broadside, as if a drunken stranger at a bar had come out of the shadows and coldcocked him.

Despite the passage of time, Ashford Connor knew well the nightmare's origins. It was less a nightmare than a rerun of the worst day of his life, a resurgence of a horrible incident in his youth that had plunged him into the darkest of places and turned him into a tormented soul. Ash had often endured the same nightmare as a teenager. They had begun soon after that sordid episode. Not every night, but off and on, without abatement, for a couple of years. But once he'd left his family as a young adult to chart his own course, the nightmares had stopped, perhaps not coincidentally.

It had been more than twenty years since the last one. But the pain he'd suffered that night, on top of the pain he'd accumulated leading to that night, marked time with him each day. His cheerful and sarcastic adult personality was but a mask. He had done an outstanding job of projecting himself as a well-adjusted, grounded person—so outstanding, in fact, that he'd succumbed to his own hyperbole, convincing himself that the demons of his youth had long taken their leave. But he recalled the actual event that fueled the nightmares as if it had occurred the day before. It was not something most people would forget, even if relegated to memory's back burner.

Now, this particular night, when the cruel nightmare reared its ugly head again, while his cherished Caitlyn slept sweetly beside him, it did not surprise him that each detail reappeared in microscopic view, and each attendant emotion he'd suffered then swelled inside him again. He knew that, indeed, he had never moved on. He had deluded himself. He was still deep in.

In the nightmare, Ash saw his teenage self in bed, on his back, in his lightless childhood bedroom. The moon, which sometimes cast a sliver of light through the window, had gone undercover, tucked behind clouds. The house had gone still. No one stirred. Not his parents, nor his sister. The clock showed 10:30 p.m.

He heard shuffling, furniture moving. Then yelling, the voices of both parents. Next, objects crashing. Then sobs, the muffled voice of his mother. Anger, from his father, the words indecipherable. He usually couldn't make them out. The doors to his and their bedroom were always shut. It did not matter. It had become a pattern. He knew what was coming next. He folded the bed pillow over his ears—and braced.

The pillow didn't help. He could hear the snap of a whip, the sound of a lashing, followed by screams, sharp sounds of anguish, which he'd heard many times before. They never got old. Each time they sounded fresh. Each time he absorbed them into his psyche, tried to make them a part of himself, steal them, dilute their power. *I will make them mine*, he'd tell himself. *Maybe that will help.*

The shrillness of his mother's anguish shook him to his core, made him physically ill and despondent, producing not only anger toward his father and fear for the well-being of his mother, but a sustained sense of futility about his own existence. He harbored grave doubts about the sheer purpose of living. He often went to bed wishing that he would not awake, that the miserable life he had been given would end. *If this is what life has to offer, why bother?*

That night, however, the night the nightmare resurfaced, something snapped inside him. The sounds were the same. The pain he imagined his mother suffering, the same. But this time they landed differently. He sat up in bed. He felt a strange force take over. He got calm. In that moment, he knew he could no longer remain passive. He had to stop being a bystander. He had to stand up for his mother—and for himself.

All of thirteen years old, Ashford Connor had crossed a Rubicon. He flung his bed sheets to the side, slid out of bed, and, with steely purpose, sprinted down the hall to his parents' bedroom in the two-story farmhouse that for generations had been the hallmark of his family lineage. The stories passed down over the years highlighted how farming life—tilling the land and celebrating simple rural values like humility, temperance, self-reliance, independence, and honor—had been the cornerstone of the Connor family identity, their pride and joy.

You get what you give. You give what you get.

But his father had severed the ancestral link to a thriving agrarian family culture. Under the iron hand of his father, the family home had become a torture chamber for a rageful alcoholic.

Ash flung open the door to his parents' bedroom so hard it smashed into the wall. His father, Patrick Benjamin Connor, who was standing menacingly over his mother lying prone on the ground, suspended his assault and snapped his head toward the door. Seeing his son, he lowered the horse whip in his hand and froze. His eyes bulged. Sweat poured off his bright-crimson face. His chest heaved from his sadistic workout.

Ash stared back with restrained anger, his fists clenched, his eyes wide, his purpose unmistakable. It was a look his father had never seen.

"You best get back to your room, Ashford—now, boy!"

Ash stood his ground and said nothing.

His father's eyes widened, betraying disbelief at what he was seeing. Patrick Benjamin Connor hesitated. Then he shuffled two steps in Ash's direction, relaxing his grip on the whip to straighten it out for use.

"Ash, honey, it's okay, please go back to your room." His mother rose to her feet. "It's okay, sweetie."

"Best you heed your mom," his father said, taking a bold step toward him.

Ash peered into his mother's eyes, wet with tears and oozing with fear.

"No. You need to stop this, now," Ash said. "This ends now." He was stunned at how relaxed the words sounded. He was channeling gobs of fear inside, but outside, he was the calm before the storm.

"You little shit. Perhaps you need a taste of this too."

Ash took two steps toward his father. "Put down the whip," he said.

His father eased the whip behind him like he was cocking a gun. Ash did not flinch. His father came at him, the whip raised. Ash stepped slightly to the side and smacked his father hard in the face, sending him to the ground, face first. He lost his hold on the whip, which flopped to the ground, stilled like a felled snake.

Ash picked up the whip and tossed it several feet away.

His father rose on one knee, shook his head as if to clear his mind. Then he got to both feet, turned, and charged Ash, who hit him square in the face with a closed fist, sending his father to the bedroom floor again, this time flat on his back.

Like a professional wrestler, Ash pounced on his father, sat on his chest, put his hands around his throat, and began to choke him. There could be no question of intent. He was choking to kill. He began to bounce his father's head up and down as he tightened his grip around his father's throat. His father's eyes bulged and reddened, and he began to regurgitate all over his chin.

"Ash, stop! Stop, you'll kill him!" his mother said.

Yes, thought Ash, *exactly. I want to kill him.*

In that moment, his sister entered the room, mouth agape, speechless. On catching sight of her, Ash stopped, released his father's head, and stood tall, straddling his father, both fists clenched. He treated him to the same menacing look that his father had tormented his mother with minutes earlier, looking down at him like he was a defeated boxer in the ring. His father lay there, struggling to return oxygen to his lungs, coughing up a storm.

"You ever put a hand on my mother again"—Ash paused to take in a breath—"I *will* kill you."

It was when he said those words that Ash awoke from the nightmare, dripping with sweat, breathing heavily. After he'd realized where he was, he glanced at Caitlyn to see if she was asleep. Thankfully, she was. He sat up in bed and wiped his brow with the back of his right hand. He eased out of bed to avoid disturbing his wife and tiptoed to the kitchen.

He went straight to the refrigerator and poured himself a glass of milk and grabbed two large chocolate chip cookies from a porcelain jar sitting in a deep corner on the kitchen counter. It took but a few minutes with Ashford Connor to learn about his fixation with chocolate chip cookies. Most colleagues and friends dismissed it as an adult indulgence or an expression of his inner child. Both perspectives held a slice of truth, but not in the way anyone imagined. The craving for chocolate chip cookies bore roots in his father's domestic abuse of his mother. When the abuse had first begun, or at least as far back as when it had begun to slowly beat down Ash, he'd resorted to chocolate chip cookies to sugarcoat his misery. As a kid, he'd stockpiled the cookies in great numbers, hiding them from everyone, like it was a drug supply. Whenever his father beat or emotionally abused his mother, he'd devour a couple of them, sometimes more. Of course, whenever he did, the fix wound up being a mixed blessing, since the sugar overload kept him up at bedtime, leaving him to suffer the pain and anguish of whatever abusive events that night had in store. He'd carried the habit—what others saw as a silly vice, but in truth, a time-honored emotional crutch—into his adult life. At the slightest provocation of stress or conflict, especially when dealing with academic and political matters at the university, he announced a desire to have a chocolate chip cookie and, if one was not available, it was all he could do not to toss a childish hissy fit.

As he stood in the kitchen after the nightmare, however, it was not the reminder of the genesis of his cookie addiction that burned inside Ash. Nearly strangling his father to death as a teenager had taught him how capable he was of killing someone with his bare hands. If his sister had not entered the room, he probably would have finished the job. He had over time pushed that awful experience deep into his consciousness. But this time, he'd experienced the nightmare differently than how he had as a child. The Ash in tonight's dream had enjoyed what he'd done, felt empowered by it. Not because his heroics had saved his mother or because he'd felt the thrill of vengeance—he'd been there before. Rather, the nightmare had unearthed something new within him. Standing over his vanquished father like a conquering gladiator in the heyday of the Roman Empire had felt familiar, as if not uncharted territory. He'd experienced it before, and worse, even, he'd felt he might even be well suited for the task—and that freaked him out.

He sat in the kitchen, munching mindlessly on a cookie, plumbing his brain for a past connection to explain the sensation. As an educator, he knew that childhood experiences could create self-images that got embedded over time, ways of seeing ourselves in the world and relative to others. He scrolled through his memory bank for movies and TV shows he'd seen growing up. Were there characters he'd identified with who engaged in violent retribution, Hollywood heroes and antiheroes he'd wanted to emulate, maybe a sheriff from the Wild West or a modern-day police officer or detective who triumphed over evil? He found nothing.

Then a light went off in his head. His subconscious and what happened with his father must have fused with his classroom lectures. He often waxed enthusiastically about his pet theory, what he dubbed the "Death Harvest Theory," which posited how instances of major human calamity precipitated notable advances in the progress of human civilization, and how those historical eras often included prolonged confrontations with barbarians, sea people, and other Darwinian manifestations of the survival of the fittest. Whenever he broached this topic, he was in his element, displaying uncommon passion about how commonplace it was hundreds of years ago to take the lives of others, and while "it might seem barbarous" to his riveted students today, in those ancient times, taking the life of another held "honor, legitimate purpose, and even romance." Ash often daydreamed about what life had been like back then, trying to understand human nature, motivation, values, and cultural nuances. *Have we really changed?* he often said to himself. *Who are we, really?*

Lost in thought that morning, he wondered if that was it. His nightmare might be some inexplicable, random convergence of what had happened with his father and his romanticizing of a barbarous era in human history. He could see how he had created for himself a historical persona that fancied the art of the kill, a hero who protected others in the quest to survive. How or why his subconscious had melded two seemingly divergent emotional sources baffled him. But perhaps there was a logical link between his academic musings and the feelings he'd experienced during the recent nightmare. In any event, the explanation satisfied him enough for the time being.

He knew one thing for sure, at least in the wee hours of the morning, alone in his kitchen—whatever the explanation for what had gone down, he was not about to tell anyone, most of all not Caitlyn. He had zero interest in taking that path. *I have a secret now*, he thought, *and that suits me fine.*

He tossed the last cookie remnant into his mouth, washed it down with what was left of his milk, and returned to bed. He had to get some shut-eye, for he had a huge day ahead.

2

CAMPUS LIFE

After managing a couple of hours sleep post-nightmare, Ash shoved the middle-of-the-night intrusion aside for the time being and geared up to confront a weighty campus dilemma beckoning on his watch.

Bradley Markowitz, a well-known conservative Fox News contributor, was scheduled to speak on campus about the Israeli-Palestinian conflict, and school officials had delegated Ash the unenviable job of facilitating the event, a natural outgrowth of his keen interest—be careful what you ask for—in developing diverse scholarship for the tenure process. In prior years, a lecture of the sort would not have drawn much attention, but recent times had stoked student groups on both sides of the political divide, with the dialogue becoming increasingly virulent and striking a fever pitch. So far as Ash and Caitlyn were concerned, their fears about the prospects of violence were not merely paranoia. They were real—the intensity between the two polarized student groups could easily combust. At their urging, the school administration had directed campus security to galvanize but had not followed their advice to ask local law enforcement for assistance. Ash and Caitlyn chastised the school's parochial decision as shortsighted and naïve. While campus security boasted a dedicated group of officers, they were hardly equipped to deal with large numbers of aggressive, undisciplined students and who-knew-what-visitors if things went off the rails. Up to this point, unchecked behavior had been minimized, but the potential for explosive violence represented a clear and present danger.

A talk show host and syndicated columnist who often appeared on Fox News, One America News, and other media outlets, Brad Markowitz brought vigor and outsize personality to political events. He delighted in using higher education as a whipping post, lambasting institutional leaders for encouraging misguided and reckless social liberalism, which he maintained undermined social institutions and made America increasingly unstable and vulnerable. His rhetoric stirred the pot of chaotic fanaticism.

Markowitz also had become a target of antisemitic Arab groups due to his political opinions on the Arab-Israeli conflict, including the territories in Judea and Samaria, which were regularly the topic of national and international news. Social media posts both supported and condemned Markowitz, sometimes with intense passion. In the past, his posts and platform had almost never raised serious safety concerns. But they had recently taken on a different flavor, more aggressive and troubling, as coverage of him widened and deepened and his brand became more popular. In recent months, he'd begun for the first time to receive death threats, as had members of his family.

Most recently, he had been invited to speak at the Graduate Center of the City University of New York, where he'd supported Israel's one-state solution. Because of the uproar surrounding the anticipated presentation, the NYPD had dispatched dozens of law enforcement personnel to ensure the speech took place as planned. An enflamed demonstration ensued on the outskirts, and while he'd delivered his remarks with no arrests or reported injuries, anti-Israeli groups had almost shouted him down. It was like water in a teapot on the verge of boiling.

If that were not troubling enough, Coronado had another professor, Abdullah Kassimali, who recently had begun to lecture on Islamic studies as part of a newly designed political science program. Kassimali, a well-known Palestinian activist, was not shy about sharing his radical political opinions on campus: "Jews are Nazis," to quote his mentor and friend, Muhammad Harzani, a well-known Hamas leader. The administration did nothing to censor or caution Professor Kassimali about inflammatory speech and open antisemitism, which unnerved Jewish and pro-Israel students.

Despite dark clouds on the horizon, the administration had failed to take steps to draw the admittedly difficult boundaries between speech that enriches debate of sensitive issues and speech that calls for unacceptable action. Because the administration seemed tone deaf—or worse, devoid of concern for student safety—as senior member of the Psychology Department, Caitlyn had requested a meeting with the administration. Ideas flowed. Many right things were said. But that was it. There was no follow-up action, other than the standard declarations supporting free speech.

The implicit tolerance for advocating for and teaching controversial topics had muddled the tenure process as well. Were inflammatory published writings that verged on encouraging or justifying violence considered sufficiently scholarly for purposes of granting tenure? The university had gone through several years of attacks on its tenure-system guidelines and had become gun-shy, fearful of stepping in and drawing deep lines in the sand. Historical standards governing tenure had yielded to ad hoc analysis and often political capriciousness. The administration seemed asleep at the switch as accountability and thoughtfully articulated standards of scholarship declined and institutional values became moving targets with no ballast. Self-advocacy reigned, and the squeaky wheel got the grease.

Initially no one had noticed the fine-grained changes to the academic system, which allowed more leeway for new and redesigned programs and courses and increased professorial freedom. But amid a struggle between basic civilities and blind adherence to the concept of unfettered academic freedom, which certain professors brandished as a guaranteed liberty, many academic boundaries floated aimlessly. The opening of the newest Islamic studies program was a case in point. A vocal professor with an unhidden political agenda had managed to usher in a large influx of Middle Eastern students and garner $15 million in grant money from foreign sources to help run the program. It had happened seamlessly, with little or no oversight.

The growth of the foreign student population coincided with an increase in cultural and religious problems on campus. The first major issue had been female Middle Eastern students who needed completely separate residential spaces to live, eat, work, and study. The dormitories could tolerate absolutely no mixing of the sexes. Separate prayer space had to be allocated during the day, and a religious leader available to ensure only Muslim students had access.

These changes, on their face, represented merely cultural mixing and adaptations. But the atmosphere had become more severe when Professor Kassimali, renowned anti-Israel activist, became a faculty member and part of the new Islamic studies program.

When Ash arrived on campus in the morning, he expected to see life as usual at that hour, mostly groggy students dragging themselves to and from class, the day slowly unfurling for everyone. He found instead large groups gathered here and there, emitting a razor-sharp buzz that threatened to blossom into a raucous roar, as everyone emoted anxiety about Bradley Markowitz's upcoming speech and how Professor Kassimali and his organization, Peace in Palestine (PIP)—the largest organized group on campus—might respond. Still, Ash was not too surprised. He knew coalition lines would be drawn eventually during the day.

But what took him aback were the flyers all over campus. One set showed a photo of Bradley Markowitz with a big, black X through his face. Another depicted photos of US politicians with long records of supporting Israel, with Stars of David etched on their foreheads and "Anti-American" written underneath each.

Before working further on his opening remarks for the Markowitz event, Ash tracked down Caitlyn. He needed consultation.

"What's happened here?" Ash said, not concealing his frustration.

"Nothing. Nothing happened, and that's the whole point," Caitlyn said.

"It has an ominous feel," Ash said.

"The President retreated to his lair and bolted the door, content to hide behind freedom-of-speech clichés. He won't do a damn thing at this point."

"How do we protect the students? I'm worried there will be a violent clash. If not tonight, then at some point in the near future." Ash's normal carefree air had taken leave.

"I know. I asked again. They won't allow police on campus. They're worried it might exacerbate things, enflame the radical ones."

Ash recalled how even the "Night of Anger" recently held on campus on Israel's Independence Day, which had resulted in widespread vandalism, had not brought any strong response or admonition from the administration. How campus life had changed! Using violence to express political views had been normalized.

They agreed to discuss the situation at home later in the day.

* * *

Caitlyn was worried. She normally leaned on Ash to tell her the sky was not falling. While he had passion and intensity to spare, underlying everything he did was a devil-may-care attitude. He did not sweat the small things, or most things, for that matter. Once he grabbed the reins, all was good. But now she saw in his face fear and worry—a new look for him, a look that told her he did not know what to do, and maybe they had been placed in a situation not only not of their making but over which they had no control. Those clouds on the horizon had moved closer to shore—they were getting larger and darker.

For quite some time, Caitlyn had been dealing with a related problem having to do with her role as a student advisor. She felt stressed about the difficulty of clarifying the ambiguous line between the responsibilities of an academic advisor and a psychological counselor. She was not a therapist. But she consistently dealt with emotionally overwrought students who were floundering over personal, family, or academic issues. As chair of the Psychology Department, Caitlyn had to maintain some distance to be an effective administrator, but the pull to help, especially in dealing with the fears of Jewish students who felt under fire, tugged at her each day. This burden weighed heavily on her as she made her way home.

* * *

Ash was awaiting her arrival in her favorite room, the kitchen, stark white with large gold tiles on the backsplash behind the sink and cabinets and on the walls around two bay windows. On the white quartz counter sat a black lacquered Jura coffee machine, which was legendary among the psychology students who had met with her in the kitchen for one reason or another. The students enjoyed watching their coveted professor's barista skills. For her part, Caitlyn was addicted to that Jura machine and to the flat white coffees she brewed every morning and every night, her fix during times of stress. Ash ate chocolate chip cookies; she drank flat white coffees.

Ash sat at the quartz counter sipping English breakfast tea and chowing down on Bob's Red Mill oatmeal cereal blended with peanut butter and topped with sliced bananas. Seeing his wife, he rose and gave her a hug.

"So, my darling, what sort of mess do we have on campus?" Ash said, not expecting a response to the rhetorical question.

Caitlyn beelined for the coffee machine. "Well, for the moment, my love, Coronado is relatively quiet. A lot of hum, but nothing disturbing," she said. "But as I left the parking lot, security was throwing barricades up along the East Campus gymnasium"—she pointed across the kitchen in the direction of the gym—"where Markowitz will present. Security guards are canvassing."

"Yeah, they had to schedule extra shifts." He smiled and nodded. "I just heard they even were forced to ask for local help."

"Right," Caitlyn said, "I got an email from Robertson that the administration finally buckled to reality. They're allowing some local police."

"Robertson? Thought the good inspector retired?"

"He did, just can't keep away, is all. He has no authority. Kind of a freelance go-between and advisor." Caitlyn flipped the switch on the coffee machine. "He thinks there's greater potential for violence because PIP has been recruiting new members for newsworthy events." Her voice was low and worried and she kept her back to him, avoiding eye contact.

Ash tilted his head to the side and squinted. "What are you not telling me?" He placed his large tablespoon down on the quartz countertop, making a loud clinking noise, and folded his arms across his chest.

Caitlyn dipped her head and then turned to face him. "Well, I guess I have to tell you sometime." She took a seat across from Ash, eyeing him carefully. "I contacted Stand with Us to help support pro-Israel students."

"What is Stand with Us?"

"Well, among other things, an advocacy organization."

"Okay."

"They work with pro-Israel students and faculty to bring Israel to campus through seminars and speakers. They teach students how to deal with antisemitism. They empower pro-Israel students so they're not intimidated by horrible accusations and behavior, including rape and the killing of women and children in Israel, the Middle East, and wherever else."

Ash nodded, waiting for more.

Caitlyn took a flyer out of her bag and read from it aloud. "Here's their mission statement: 'Stand with Us is an international nonprofit Israel education organization, established in 2001. We are inspired by our love of Israel, by our belief that education is the road to peace, and by our commitment to stand up for Israel and the Jewish people when they are publicly attacked or misrepresented.'"

Ash did not respond.

"What could be better for our students?" Caitlyn said. "Joshua Weiss, my doctoral student, told me that introducing him to Stand with Us was the best thing I ever did for him, as well as several of his friends and colleagues.

"In any case, representatives from Stand with Us have met with me and about fifty students in the Student Union to discuss campus strategy for today's protest. We've been making plans for organizing more students on campus to offset the awful materials that Kassimali's PIP group has disseminated. We have a plan to support Markowitz's lecture today and stamp out any heckling."

Ash understood Caitlyn well enough to know she would do what she needed to do. And he trusted her judgment. But why had she kept that information from him? Did she not trust him? In fairness, had she told him what she was planning, he likely would have pushed back. The more the students coalesced, no matter how well-intentioned or necessary, the greater the heat and the more likely things would turn violent. Then again, how much control did they have in the current situation? It had all the signs of a raging snowball barreling down the mountain, expanding exponentially in size and threatening to become a catastrophic avalanche. For the first time, he felt fear, real fear. Still, he knew he'd better stay even-keeled.

"Okay. Sounds good. Let's make sure we're on the same page—please. Don't forget, we're *both* involved with the Markowitz event, and I'm introducing him to the audience. I will do what I can to caution everyone to be courteous and respectful and make clear that disruptive outbursts will likely result in expulsion from the gym."

Caitlyn's iPhone pinged. She dropped her eyes to the screen. "It's a text from Inspector Robertson. Professor Kassimali intends to hold a rally with PIP on the main campus in front of the Humanities building. Barriers will be set up to control things, prevent vandalism."

She drew a long, deep breath. "The campus is about to get crazy. There'll be news reporters and cameras everywhere. Why did President Brightson permit Kassimali to hold a rally today? Why didn't he put Kassimali off, even for a day or two?" She shook her head a few times and grimaced.

"Caitlyn, let's be honest. The Coronado administration is sympathetic to the Kassimali cause. How do you think antisemitism has flourished on campuses for years? Hell, look at Harvard now, Columbia, NYU, Berkeley. It's like a rampant virus."

Ash drained the rest of his tea and set his cup on the table. His chest felt tight. He got up from his chair and inhaled and exhaled deeply through his nose, raised and dropped his shoulders. "I need a cookie."

"While you're up, Ash, can you make me another flat white coffee?"

3

CAMPUS POLITICS

By eight a.m., an hour prior to the event, the line to enter had snaked beyond eyesight, a steady procession ready to present IDs to a uniformed security guard at the main entrance of Coronado's gymnasium. Two TV news crews had set up inside earlier, at designated courtside areas at opposite ends of the gym. Caitlyn had organized a group of nearly a hundred students, who had arrived early and were commandeering seats in the front rows of the bleachers near the center of the gym, on one side of the grandstand. Many sported signs and posters. For most students, this would be their maiden rally and protest voyage, and their unease was palpable as they piled into the gym. Caitlyn grabbed a seat in the middle, a few rows back from the elevated podium, to provide moral support. Several other faculty and administrators sat in a small, self-conscious, carefully separate group near the front of the student audience.

Professor Abdullah Kassimali entered the gym wearing a conservative tweed suit and dark red tie with blue stripes as he tried to blend in with students in the near center of a row near the top of the grandstand. Being inconspicuous was not, however, an option for him. His shoulder-length hair and thick, black beard alone distinguished him. But there was something else about him, a fiery glow that signaled storms brewing and a face that combined a roguish smile with the studied countenance of a keen observer. He scanned the gym with beady eyes while speaking softly to some students.

If anyone was not eager upon arrival, the frenetic buzz in the gym would fix that.

A platform and podium had been erected on the gym floor, a few feet in front of the crowded seats at the gym center, and a handful of security police were standing along the open areas at the edge of the court. As nine a.m. approached, it was standing room only, and when Ash appeared on stage to kick off the event and introduce the speaker, everyone took their seats on cue, filling them all.

The buzz reduced slightly, became more a persistent murmur, which prompted Ash to raise a hand to signal a request for silence and attention. To his surprise, like air out of a balloon, the gym noise vaporized. The entire gym quieted, an abrupt and eerie silence that knocked him a little off center. He cleared his throat conspicuously before speaking.

"Good morning, everyone—and, um, welcome. As most of you know, I am Professor Ashford Connor, and I have the privilege of introducing our speaker this morning."

Ash scanned the audience for a few seconds. Although quiet remained, he felt a strange vibe. Maybe his nerves.

"Before we get started with this part of our speaker program, I want to make a few comments." Again he paused, this time looking straight ahead. "As you can see, television cameras are here, and we, of course, welcome them. We are proud of the educational tradition at Coronado University—and we are proud today to kick off a robust and solemn educational experience consistent with that tradition. Please be mindful that each of you is an integral part of what will happen today and at subsequent events in this speaker series, and that will reflect on our identity and reputation in the larger community." When Ash saw nods in the audience, he nodded in kind, moving his head in a half-circle to scan the room.

"School officials are quite aware . . . that today's subject matter can invoke passion and even controversy. The school acknowledges, and welcomes, the exchange of heartfelt and well-considered contrary viewpoints. Listening with respect and openness to both sides of a debate on matters of social and political importance is the hallmark of a vibrant and distinguished educational culture. Consistent with the history of the school, we expect everyone to listen and consider thoughtfully what they hear and observe a polite decorum for what will be the first of many lectures on different topics that challenge us today in our complex world."

Ash scanned the audience to gauge the reaction from the multitudes. It was hard to tell—the collection of faces betrayed more uncertainty than focus and engagement—but he took note that no one booed or hissed or threw anything at him. That was some comfort. No matter, it was time to get on with it.

"We are fortunate today to have Bradley Markowitz, a conservative news commentator and distinguished lecturer who has traveled throughout the world and lectured on many controversial issues facing our communities and country. As many of you know, Mr. Markowitz is also a talk show host and syndicated columnist who often appears on various media outlets and is *The New York Times* bestselling author of *Taming the Middle East: There's But One Solution*."

The mention of the controversial book triggered low-grade hums in a few spots around the gym, the kind of rumbling that often preceded spirited boos. Ash moved on quickly.

"Please all welcome Mr. Markowitz to Coronado University."

Bradley Markowitz had been standing near the gym entrance. On cue, he strode across the floor with long, confident steps and mounted the stage. He wore a high-quality vested suit tailored to showcase his fit, medium-height frame. His shoulder-length black hair hung with a sheen under his *kippah*—a skullcap—a new look for many of the assembled students who'd never met an Orthodox Jew, let alone had an opportunity to hear one address a controversial topic like the survival of the State of Israel.

Ash shook his hand and walked off stage, a little too eagerly. Markowitz put down his case, adjusted the microphone, and cleared his throat. Before he could speak, however, students in the middle rows began to yell obscenities and wave anti-Israel placards. The scattered shouts continued nonstop for minutes, stealing the moment, before a disciplined chant overwhelmed the gym.

"Free Palestine!" they chanted. "From the river to the sea, Palestine will be free."

Signs waved rhythmically. The chanting students, about twenty-five in number, rose from their seats and surged into the aisles, coalescing toward the podium.

"Free Palestine! From the river to the sea, Palestine will be free."

Campus security guards moved in against the chanting students and tried to corral them toward a side exit door. Their efforts had no impact on the chanting.

"Free Palestine! From the river to the sea, Palestine will be free."

Abdullah Kassimali stood and applauded while chanting along with the rest, smiling broadly at his young, obedient acolytes in the rows below him. He called out to them, urging some of them by name and smiling when they turned and waved up at him.

"Free Palestine! From the river to the sea, Palestine will be free."

Security guards pushed the disruptive students back up the aisles, admonishing them to return to their seats and threatening arrest. One student pulled away from the grip of a security guard and shoved the guard, who fell back and hit his head on the ground. The student thrust his fist into the air.

TV news cameras zeroed in on the mayhem.

But then something unusual occurred. The students in the three front rows, many of whom Caitlyn had brought to the event, rose and slipped into the aisle. They formed a wall, like a mobile dam, and began to force the outnumbered protestors into retreat, pushing them toward a side exit. They managed to get the protestors out of the gym without physical engagement—a small miracle, since violence had seemed inevitable. Once the protestors were shown the door, the chants subsided and the gym became eerily quiet.

Ash had campus security posted at all entrances as the chanting resumed outside, a faint and distant noise. After order was restored, he returned to the podium to join the invited speaker and asked the nervous audience to settle down and retake their seats.

"Mr. Markowitz, apologies. Please begin."

Markowitz thanked Ash and flashed a wide smile to his audience. "Good morning, everyone. Passion without violence is lifeblood." He paused for a few seconds to let his comment on what had transpired land.

"I am honored to visit with you on campus and speak about an issue whose resolution has evaded world leaders for decades. The Israeli-Palestinian conflict has been debated and fought since the establishment of the State of Israel. For seventy years, the United States, Israel, and the United Nations have proposed a two-state solution, with two independent countries living side by side in peace and harmony. For seventy years, Israel and the United States have tried countless times to invite Palestinian leaders to the bargaining table to resolve the conflict and create two separate states. But to no avail. Palestinians have spurned these efforts, electing instead to do what they can to eliminate the State of Israel with a barrage of violence, including missile attacks, border violations, Intifada incursions, and thousands and thousands of rockets."

He spread his arms in an elegant shrug and lowered his voice, as if sharing a secret with friends at a private meeting. "Israel has learned during those seventy years that there exists no peace partner in Palestinian leadership. That, in a nutshell, is why a two-state solution is a waste of time."

He looked around the audience and nodded to himself. "Today, I propose to you a one-state solution. I am aware it remains controversial, but I believe the United States will ultimately back the one-state solution as the only viable answer to the present situation. It is far superior to perpetual war. The killing must stop." Markowitz leaned back and delivered the next comment with a slightly raised voice. "Most Israelis fear that an independent Palestinian state could potentially militarize and invade Israel along its continuous adjacent border. Their fears are well grounded, and that cannot be allowed."

He opened his hands and reached out to the audience for understanding. "A one-state solution would create a federation with Palestinian cantons inside Israel, just like in Switzerland. They would have political and social, but not military, autonomy. The Israeli Defense Forces would maintain security inside that federation. Order and normal living would be restored."

He lowered his gaze to focus on some students in the front row who were starting to whisper to each other. "The primary concern under any plan is population growth. Israel cannot risk getting overrun by a growing Arab population, so this plan would not have a 'right of return' to the Israeli cantons. Palestinians would stay where they are presently or leave Israel. Israel would remain a strictly Jewish state, precisely as its Arab neighbors are Muslim, but would remain the only democracy in the Middle East." For the next twenty minutes, he expanded on his proposal with particulars about living arrangements, the economy, schools and education, the arts and culture, language, and medical services and health care.

When he concluded his prepared remarks, he invited questions. There were many. Students politely took turns. Mini-conversations ensued. By all appearances, the students had enjoyed Markowitz's dry humor, self-deprecating presentation, and natural ability to relate across the generations. He had not talked down to them but spoke directly, engaging them throughout his presentation.

After two hours, Ash brought everything to a close, thanked Markowitz, and thanked everyone for their attentive and civil behavior, ignoring what had occurred at the top. As the audience exited, Ash took Markowitz to a secluded office inside the gym. The original plan was for the controversial speaker to change into student-looking garb so if things got too heated, he could blend in with a group of students and exit without difficulty. They were about to scuttle that plan, since things had worked out without much tension, when word got back to them that a large crowd had formed outside with Professor Kassimali, and the energy was hot.

Markowitz changed out of his tie and jacket and into an old "Coronado University" hooded sweatshirt and a red ball cap, worn backward, and hung a backpack half full of books over his shoulder. Ash escorted him to a rarely used exit, where a student group dressed like Markowitz waited, and they said their goodbyes. As Markowitz slinked into the crowd, Ash could hear the Kassimali crowd getting louder.

* * *

That evening, Caitlyn made her way home and started dinner. She expected that Ash would be back later than usual—he'd had to stay a little longer on campus to brief the President on the Markowitz event. As dinnertime approached, though, Caitlyn had not heard from him. She began to worry. She knew her man was never, ever late for anything, particularly dinner. Her imagination ran wild, and she began to contrive various scenarios to explain Ash's tardiness. She turned on the TV to check in on a news station just as a Channel 5 News reporter was starting to report on a stabbing on the Coronado University East Campus quadrangle.

Campus Politics

"Bradley Markowitz, the well-known conservative political commentator and social activist, was stabbed right here on the campus quadrangle of Coronado University a little more than six hours ago. He's in the hospital. His condition is unknown at this time. Law enforcement, which has been characteristically tight-lipped, has told us little. What we do know is that the stabbing occurred in the wake of two political speeches, one by Bradley Markowitz about foreign affairs in the Middle East, which was organized by the school as part of its educational curriculum and took place inside the school gym, and the other by a schoolteacher, Professor Abdullah Kassimali, which occurred outside on campus and was apparently a counterpoint to the Markowitz talk.

"Law enforcement also told us that Markowitz's speech was initially delayed by a near-riot and a few dozen organized rioters had to be cleared out of the gymnasium before the speaker could start. It is unclear whether the second speech and protest was impromptu or planned, and if so, by whom. They would not tell us if there were any suspects but did tell us that they've made no arrests at this time.

"According to students with whom I have spoken, Professor Kassimali had been speaking for an hour when students began shouting slogans, chanting in unison, dumping garbage pails, and throwing trash at other students walking on the quadrangle lawn and streets. According to at least three student witnesses, while this was happening, Bradley Markowitz was spotted and surrounded by unknown protestors from the Kassimali gathering and apparently stabbed in the chest. He is being treated in the emergency room at Highland Memorial Hospital."

Ash entered the house and practically stumbled into the kitchen, looking dazed. He had bruises on his face and neck.

"Jesus, Ash, what happened to you?"

He plopped into a kitchen chair, his face drawn and sad. He had just come from being interviewed by law enforcement, he told her. He'd been pummeled in the melee that had led to the stabbing. "I'm angry and frustrated I couldn't do anything more to save him. I was neutralized by the damned crowd and it was all my fault—"

"What do you mean, *saved* him?"

Ash gave her a puzzled look. "Caitlyn, Bradley Markowitz is dead."

"Oh my God," she gasped. "The news reported only a stabbing, that doctors were treating him. Th-they gave no indication—"

"He was murdered by that damned Kassimali crowd . . . stabbed wantonly, like in a prison killing on TV. He didn't have a chance. I couldn't get to him in time to do anything." Ash put his face in his hands.

Caitlyn kissed his forehead and put her hands on his shoulders. He sat up and held her.

"What should we be doing?" she said.

Ash shrugged. "What can we do?" He released himself and said, "I need a shower."

"Dinner?"

"Not hungry." And off he went.

Caitlyn went to the master bedroom, undressed and slid into her long, white Neiman Marcus nightgown, fluffed the pillows, and got into bed.

Ten minutes later, Ash exited the bathroom, struggling to maintain his balance.

"Ash, are you okay? What's wrong?"

"They gave me a sedative. I'll be fine." He crawled into bed, pulled the covers over himself, and closed his eyes.

"Jesus, Ash, I can't believe he's dead. I can't get it straight in my mind." Caitlyn pulled her hair out of its scrunchie.

Her iPhone pinged. She read the text from the school President, and then gently shook Ash's shoulder. "Hey, Ash, the President's texting. He wants to know how you're feeling. He says he's been talking to the police and the family. The family doesn't want an autopsy, which is a problem for the investigation. Markowitz's wife wants the body shipped to New York for services immediately."

"I'm not up for talking," Ash whispered, keeping his eyes closed. "I'm too upset to think clearly. Tell him I'm fine—and not to worry, he won't lose his job over this."

She conveyed the message, except the last part, to the President.

"Caitlyn Morrys Connor, I love you. Now turn out the light. We can discuss blame and forgiveness in the morning."

Ash lay on his back with eyes closed, but he stayed awake for more than an hour, his mind reeling from the day's extraordinary happenings. Unable to resist the compelling search for answers and meaning, he repeatedly replayed each segment of his day leading up to the tragedy. But he failed to divine any core truth, anything that shed light on the why of it all. Confused and exhausted, his normally sharp mind was suffering a breakdown.

Except for an initial hiccup in the program, which had been handled quickly, the day had started well. Simple enough. But then it had erupted into terror and violence. Had that been inevitable? And what was it about this institution of higher learning that it had the distinction of hosting two murders in the span of a few years? And not just any garden-variety local homicides, buried inside the local newspaper. They were political assassinations.

Were they mere coincidences? Were they connected to some greater plan hovering in the universe? What would Caitlyn say? Surely, she'd have some metaphysical explanation tied up in past-life regression. Ash was not ready to go there, not with her, not with anyone. It was all he could do to wrap his head around the brutal reality of a murder to which he was at least psychically connected.

But something else nagged at him and dominated his muddled thinking. During the campus melee, when all hell had broken loose and ripened into a fever pitch that had led to the murder, rather than recoil and retreat and try his hand as peacemaker, he'd welcomed the physical engagement. He'd enjoyed it. He'd craved it. In fact, the riot had seemed eerily familiar to him, a place he'd been before, a space where he felt comfortable and righteous. It had invigorated him. *Why? Who am I, really?* Even more perplexing, as he lay in bed, eyes still closed, the love of his life sleeping next to him, he realized he wanted more.

4

THE CHOCOLATE CHIP COMMITTEE

Ash arrived about fifteen minutes early for the next meeting of the University Personnel Committee, needing time alone to collect his thoughts and brace for what he feared might be a contentious session. Upon entering the meeting room, he did what he always did—checked to see if his assistant had stocked the place with a bounty of chocolate chip cookies. And there they were, placed on a table in the corner of the room, under a lithograph he had hung when he became committee chair. It read: "In the Cookies of Life, Friends Are the Chocolate Chips." While everyone, including Caitlyn, had dismissed the cookie obsession as a harmless, childish quirk, it had become so self-identifying that under Ash's leadership, the UPC had been dubbed the Chocolate Chip Committee.

The UPC's recent work had labored under a dark cloud, marred by a top-down political agenda that had a stranglehold on the process, just as it had when Caitlyn Morrys had served as its chair. Led by President Richard Uzinski, the administrative powers-that-be had shackled the UPC with draconian "academic reforms" that marginalized school tenure in an effort to dilute the educational curriculum with regressive content. Those efforts most likely would have succeeded had Uzinski not met his maker, the victim of a heinous homicide in his office—the result, it turned out, of festering bad blood within the administration, rooted in past-life relationships.

Amid the political shenanigans, Caitlyn had left her mark as a ferocious advocate of tenure and academic freedom, paying homage to the university's prized motto, "Publish or Perish," and supporting young, struggling professors who exhibited an abiding passion for learning, scholarship, and deepening knowledge. She'd paid a price for her vigilance. The process had burned her out, prompting her to pass the tenure mantle to Ash. While her partner brought a markedly different leadership style, most notably his impatience and unfiltered sarcasm, the two shared an academic idealism and sense of collegial justice and fairness.

Unfortunately, under Ash's leadership, the UPC had failed to promote a single tenure candidate to successful conclusion. Like Caitlyn before him, Ash had toiled under the administration's tactic of cajoling department heads to hire junior faculty as "clinical" professors and part-time adjunct professors on annual contracts. That ploy foreclosed consideration of tenure for new hires and, worse, elbowed them outside the jurisdiction of the teachers' union. Worthy candidates routinely suffered the bludgeon of administrative veto power.

A batting record of zero had the expected demoralizing effect throughout the school, creating a repressive academic environment among the faculty. Many had begun to question their loyalty to the institution and direction as college professors. Teacher turnover rates had hit record-high levels. The situation screamed for a sea change or, at the least, a positive tenure decision. To say that would be easier said than done, in the current circumstances, would be a gross understatement.

The faculty member next up for tenure happened to be the campus figure at whom moral outrage over the murder of Bradley Markowitz was now directed: Professor Abdullah Kassimali from the Islamic Center.

Sitting alone in the conference room, his nerves uncharacteristically frayed, Ash considered tabling Kassimali's candidacy until cooler heads prevailed on campus and the long shadow of what had happened to Markowitz faded. There was precedent for delaying tenure applications, most commonly when the committee needed more time to gather information. Chairperson Connor could make up a viable excuse. But no matter how clever a justification he crafted, he was savvy enough to know that many would label the postponement a pretextual disguise of partisan vengeance for what had happened to Markowitz. That would only inflame things. No, he reasoned, the UPC should proceed in the ordinary course. Let the chips fall where they may.

As Ash sat there, pondering the possibilities, committee members shuffled into the room right on time. Normally a collection of chatterboxes, they took their seats around the table in moribund silence, exchanging somber nods, as if easing into the aisles of a funeral home during a wake. Ash did not like what he saw. His colleagues wanted no part of this meeting, not this day, anyway.

"Good morning, everyone. Before we get started with our next candidate, I want to make a few comments."

Heads rose and eyes gazed at their chairperson, surveying his countenance.

"What we do as a committee is not some check-the-box process to make sure all is in order, like bankers poring over a loan application. This committee is the cornerstone of an academically free and diverse educational program."

Many nodded.

"To that extent, we have failed."

To this, no one nodded, but many eyes scanned the room to see how others reacted.

"Not everyone may admit this, but it is difficult not to feel pressure to right the ship. But we have standards that guide our work. We are bound by a higher purpose than an individual agenda. We must shut out the self-serving noise that surrounds us. The integrity of this school and its academic mission require no less."

Ash paused, surprised himself at the words that had spilled from his lips. He believed them, deeply, and he knew Caitlyn would be proud of his unplanned exposition, but now that he had taken an embedded, principled stand, he was unsure where to go next—and he knew why.

As perverse as it might sound to many, Kassimali had all the makings of a poster child for the resurgence of tenure. In a normal world, Professor Kassimali, a larger-than-life personality with a strong student following, could not have been a more fitting applicant. Recommending him for tenure could allow the committee to rise above the fray. On the other hand, given the volatile situation on campus, the timing could not have been worse. Like it or not, his candidacy had become a political hot potato.

To state the obvious, Professor Kassimali was no ordinary tenure candidate. He was a Palestinian activist embroiled in an explosive campus controversy that had led to the murder of someone who espoused opposite views. Generally, political disputes fell outside the reach of the UPC, but in light of how enflamed the political climate was, and how emotional and divisive the Palestinian-Israeli conflict, it would be foolish to think the sociopolitical backdrop would not be raised. It had all the earmarks of an elephant in the room, demanding a seat at the table.

The typical review process took several weeks and involved individual interviews with students, colleagues, professors from other universities, and administrators. Two or three committee members were assigned to conduct the interviews, and the inquiries focused on the potential for excellence in teaching, research, and service to the institution, as well as identifying and critiquing existing publications and the potential for future publications. Once the results were reported to the committee, a round-table discussion among committee members would ensue, leading to a vote on what recommendation to make to the administration, which was the final arbiter.

"Let's cut to the chase," Ash said. "Let's have the positive. Who wants to start?"

Professor Sydney Sadowsky raised his clenched left hand, index finger jutting skyward. Sadowsky was tall and husky, with a white shirt and elbow-patched Ralph Lauren sweater his daughter had purchased for him on Rodeo Drive in Beverly Hills, the most expensive item in a wardrobe that generally consisted of Duluth jeans and cowboy boots. He had short, wavy hair, bushy eyebrows, black eyes, and a long mustache, which he twirled when he spoke. He was a prodigious mathematician and commanded respect among faculty and students. He saw the world in formulaic terms, leaving little room for jocularity.

He spoke in a robotic tone. "Well, to begin, every professional we spoke to sang Kassimali's praises for his activism in Ramallah and the West Bank of Israel and his positive contributions to social justice and Palestinian self-actualized statehood. He brings a passion and commitment to his teachings unmatched by most faculty."

"Students?" Ash said, exhibiting no desire to follow up.

"There, too, he got high marks. Students enjoy his teachings about progressivism and world politics. Feedback consistently affirmed his vast knowledge."

"You are saying no students criticized him. I find that hard to believe," Professor Barbara Prentice said, leaning toward Professor Sadowsky. Tall, stately, and distinguished, with silver hair tied in a neat bun, in her late sixties, Prentice had been in the School of Nursing for thirty years, and before that, a combat trauma nurse with the US Air Force. Her large gray eyes and wire-rimmed glasses divided a long, angular face engraved with war stories and grim events too serious and tragic to be fully appreciated by the average academic.

"No, I was getting to that—if I may," Sadowsky said, with genuine politeness.

Prentice leaned back in her seat.

"We interviewed over one hundred students from Professor Kassimali's classes. There were two distinct groups of students, American and foreign born. The American students stressed how Kassimali framed his curriculum around his one-sided political views on the Middle East, and because of that, they feared challenging them in class. In addition—"

"Hold on, hold on," Professor Michael Rogers said. "Why were they afraid? Did he prevent them from speaking up in any way? Did he not encourage opposite viewpoints?" The head of the Biology Department, in his fifties, the rambunctious Rogers sported wire-rimmed glasses resting loosely on his nose. He was completely bald on top, with a ring of red fuzz on the sides and back of his head. Bright-blue eyes and a very pink complexion gave him a pixie-like quality that attracted everyone. He was known for his vivid stories, constant fumbling with his elusive glasses, and an explosive sense of humor. His students loved his classes and silly jokes. His main fault was an admitted inability to suffer fools.

"Well, not that we heard," Sadowsky said in response. "They acknowledged that he invited other viewpoints. It was just how they apparently felt."

"How they *felt*?" Rogers said. "So, let me see if I understand this. We are going to give him negative marks because some snowflake students lack the self-confidence to speak their minds on a controversial topic in class, while they vomit their views all over social media? Is that what we are saying? Is that our standard for self-advocacy?"

"Down, boy," Ash said. "We are only getting reports now. Try listening. It can do wonders."

"And *I* am *only* clarifying them," Rogers said. "Careless innuendo can destroy people."

"Please continue, Professor Sadowsky," Ash said, with a shake of his head that did not conceal his disdain.

"Many students noted—"

"Which students?" Rogers said, oblivious to the dirty look from Ash.

"The American students."

"Thank you."

"As I was saying, many students noted that the courses in the Islamic Center sooner or later came down to a pro-Palestinian perspective, with a negative viewpoint on Israel and US support of Israel historically. They were sympathetic but wanted to see the other side of the issues vetted. Some complained about the absence of a course with a counter viewpoint."

"So, to be clear, if the school *offered* a course with a counter viewpoint, they would have no issue with what Professor Kassimali teaches, correct?" Rogers said.

Professor Sadowsky paused, pulled at his mustache, and glared at Rogers.

"I take that as a yes," Rogers said.

"Professor Rogers, try to listen before judging, as taxing as that may be," Ash said. "Professor Sadowsky?"

"Yes, thank you. I should add that some students—*American* students—worried that Professor Kassimali's bias was so intractable, he was antisemitic."

"Oh, for crying out loud," Rogers said. "Based on what?"

"Some mentioned anti-Christian rhetoric in history courses."

"Oh, so the history of Christianity—the Crusades, the Inquisition, the witch hunts, the Reformation, to name a few—is unblemished? Is that what this is coming down to?" Rogers said.

"Anything else, Professor Sadowsky?" Ash said, the impatience rising in his voice.

"No."

"Thank you for the hard work and professionalism... and tolerance," Ash said, casting a look at Rogers. He exhaled. He didn't want to hear from Rogers. But he had no choice. "Do you have anything to add from *your* interviews?"

"Yes, as a matter of fact. I'll be brief. I interviewed mostly foreign students. They were overwhelmingly positive about his classes, his fairness, and his value to the school. It seems to me that, putting politics aside, which, I assume from our esteemed chair's introductory speech, is how we should be guided, Professor Kassimali's teaching prowess is beyond reproach."

Ash gave Rogers a long look. "Who did the work on Kassimali's colleagues?" he asked, slowly turning his gaze away from Rogers.

"I did," said Prentice.

"Were the faculty split into two groups, like the students?" Ash asked.

"Yes. I interviewed twenty-five faculty members outside of the Islamic Center who had either taught with Professor Kassimali or worked directly with him on university projects or committees. The faculty reviews and interviews were generally positive. This group of faculty members said Kassimali was passionate about his work in the Islamic Center and committed to his students. They also indicated he was extremely opinionated and they avoided discussing politics with him. Several female colleagues who were left off committees he chaired perceived that he preferred working with males—"

"Perceived?" Rogers said. "What the hell does that mean? Sounds like disgruntled colleague character assassination."

"Two said he had a short fuse," Prentice continued. "He sometimes lost his temper and could be harsh and verbally abusive."

"Unreal," Rogers said.

"Okay, one more. Professor Curtiss, what do you have?" Ash said.

Megan Curtiss was short and heavy, with cropped blonde hair pulled to the side and behind her ears. She wore tortoiseshell glasses over a round, puffy face and a navy-blue blazer over white slacks and loafers. She was from Toronto, Canada, with a doctorate in social work. She directed the school's breast cancer program and spoke in short decisive bursts, a habit from her eight years as a military officer in the Canadian Army. She spoke without notes.

"I interviewed faculty in the Islamic Center. Everyone—understandably—raved about Professor Kassimali. Some consider him a close friend and mentor, dating from before their time at Coronado University. Many had connections to him and his family in Ramallah. They were particularly devoted to him and affirmed their loyalty to his political cause. Most had taken courses with him in Ramallah, and some had received training directly from him. Some said the Islamic Center program could not survive without him."

"Thank you." Ash nodded and smiled for the first time during the meeting.

"Who handled the administrators?"

"I did," Professor Christian Rudman said, raising his hand. A popular teacher in the School of Business and a triathlete, Rudman hailed from Raleigh, North Carolina. He'd run several midsize businesses before embarking on a college teaching career. Rudman was muscular and of average height, with a buzz haircut. He had dark eyes, round, black designer glasses, and a short-cropped, well-groomed beard.

"I have letters and interview reports from two academic deans and the Provost. The deans were complimentary about Kassimali and the addition of the Islamic Center to the curriculum. They did not see a problem with any other students, or any Jewish students in particular. When I mentioned how many Jewish students had complained about the BDS movement—Boycott, Divestment, and Sanctions—and how some of them had even left Coronado University, they denied any knowledge of that occurring. Apparently, no one on campus has complained directly to them about the Islamic Center, or at least, that's how they told it."

"Anything else?"

"Yes, the Provost was beside himself in praising the financial contributions Kassimali has made to the university. That was all he wanted to talk about."

"Okay. Thanks, everyone. The main issue I see concerns publications," Ash said. "In the entire time I have sat on this committee, dating back to when Professor Morrys was chair, we have never—*never*—recommended anyone for tenure without some meaningful publications to their credit."

"Well, there is a first for everything," Rogers said.

"Perhaps, Professor Rogers, but maybe you've forgotten that the tenure criteria include publications—"

"Well—"

"I'm not finished, Professor Rogers. At this university, tenure requires a minimum of ten publications over five years, or twelve peer-reviewed articles in top journals, just like you have accomplished, Professor Rogers, and impressively, I might add—"

"Yes, but—"

"I'm still not finished. Professor Kassimali has not authored a single textbook or contributed curriculum content to any academic anthology. Nor, evidently, is anything in that ballpark in the planning stage. His body of published work includes a smattering of articles in fringe online magazines that cater to radical politics."

"Ah, yes, Professor Connor, I am disappointed in you. You are missing the most important point."

"Oh, is that so?"

"It's called money. Professor Kassimali is directly responsible for millions of dollars in grants to the university from Qatar and Saudi Arabia, as well as the positive press the school received from his fundraising efforts. We all should be grateful for how he's kept us afloat during tough times. Let's not look a gift horse in the mouth."

The room grew still. All eyes turned to Ash.

"I need a chocolate chip cookie," Ash said.

5

OUT OF THE FRYING PAN . . .

Before he realized it, Ash had started chomping on his second cookie. He hardly remembered devouring the first one, which he'd consumed like a vacuum cleaner as his mind ricocheted every which way, up, down, and sideways, as if he were on a roller coaster contorted in the shape of a pretzel. For the first time since he'd become chair of the committee, he was at a loss to provide leadership and direction in making this decision.

Were he operating on an even playing field, paying homage to established tenure rules, he'd put the kibosh on the Kassimali candidacy. Time and again, he could righteously hammer on a fundamental tenure requirement: publications. The man had not published anything remotely deserving of academic distinction and in all likelihood never would. He didn't conduct academic research. His body of work . . . well . . . it didn't exist. When it came to this aspect of the process, Kassimali was a different kind of professorial force—the antithesis of collegiate scholarship.

Ash could not recall any past candidates who'd been so out of touch with the pure academic standards expected of faculty members vying for tenure. Sure, Kassimali was passionate, charismatic, bright, and well-versed in the subject matter of his courses. Sure, he could boast a loyal student following. But he shrouded his teaching agenda in political messaging and lacked even a semblance of a balanced approach to his subject and delivery of facts. Viewed in that light, the decision should be easy. Based on express, objective institutional standards, he did not qualify.

But each time Ash landed there, he shivered as he thought about the political ramifications of turning Kassimali away, even though he had little doubt that if they took that bold step, the President would backhand their recommendation and grant tenure anyway. *Show me the money.* That was what the administration was all about.

And the optics mattered, didn't they? A presidential override of the committee's "no" recommendation would grant the committee some cover with the anti-Palestinian segments on campus, casting them as loyal standard-bearers of a pristine tenure process. In contrast, recommending tenure would score rare points with the administration, but would enflame festering fears in the Jewish student body and their supporters, who were operating on the thinnest of edges.

No matter how he sliced it, the politics took the committee—if not overtly, then sub silentio—outside the bounds of the traditional playbook. It was, as best he could tell, a classic "damned if you do, damned if you don't" conundrum.

But he couldn't avoid taking a stand, somewhere. He had a strong urge to call Caitlyn to get her take. But he knew what she would say. She had told him before. *Stick to the criteria. Be pure. You are duty bound to the system. You have a mandate. Block out the noise.* Defaulting to her would, in truth, be a way to rest his troubled head on her strong shoulders. It would be an expression of weakness, an implicit admission that he was not cut out for the job, that he was more bluster than substance. And worse, that maybe he was not the man he'd seemed to be when he stood up to his father. No, he had made this bed, and he should lie in it. He had to go it alone.

Ash continued to process in rapid fashion. He couldn't prevent himself from asking a question he knew he shouldn't ask, much less answer. But at this point, he was scrambling for a lifeline. Nothing was off the table. *Which group do I want to piss off the least?*

He wolfed down the last large chunk of cookie and braced himself to call the meeting back to order. As he walked back into the room, he noticed Professor Rogers and several other committee members huddled in a corner in animated conversation.

"Okay, let's get back to business and take everyone's temperature," Ash said. "Let's have an informal, noncommittal vote to see where we are at this juncture."

A straw vote, while not unprecedented, was not the norm. Ash had opted for baby steps, a play-it-by-ear approach—draw people out before he put his foot into the water. He distributed a batch of voting sheets around the room. No one as much as peeked at anyone else, each marking and folding the sheet with eyes lowered and then passing their vote down the table to Ash in collective silence.

"Okay, let's see what we have. Hmm. Five 'no' votes and five 'yes' votes," Ash said, crunching his brow.

"That's only ten, Ashford. Did you forget to vote?" Professor Rogers said.

"Mine will come later. Let's discuss," Ash said, cutting to the chase. "We have a candidate who does not meet the publication requirements, or even come close, and who is a mixed bag when it comes to how the student body receives him. And contrary to what the President and Professor Rogers may think, fundraising prowess is not a tenure criterion. So, what gives with the five affirmatives? What are people thinking?"

"I'll tell you," Professor Rogers said.

Ash nodded at Rogers.

"I take exception to what you said. It is true that our tenure manual"—Rogers thrust his copy above his head—"does not refer to fundraising as such. But it does cite the following factor as part of what we should consider, and I quote: 'the potential to *contribute significantly* to the mission of the university.' I ask you, can there be a more significant contribution to our mission than delivering copious funds that keep our doors open, keep us employed and assure our students have classes to attend? Especially in turbulent times, when the very foundation of the institution is threatened? We should be grateful he is among us and wants to drop an anchor. And I don't mind saying, we should get off our high horses and stop spewing platitudes about academic this or that when we have someone in front of us to whom we should be eternally grateful for our jobs. Let's stop with the ceremonial nonsense and be the adults in the room."

"Anything else?" Ash said, trying to keep from wincing.

"Yes. I think it is unfair to call his student record a 'mixed bag,' unless, of course, we are allowing political allegiances to impact our recommendation, which I know Mr. Chairperson would never allow. It is a so-called mixed bag because the subject matter he teaches of necessity invites partisan viewpoints. *Not* because he is not an excellent instructor."

"Any response?" Ash said.

"I have one," Susan Rothchild said, usually quiet in the committee meetings. "Let me begin with what I think is a rhetorical question. Does anyone have any evidence of a faculty member getting tenure primarily based on their fundraising record for the school? Has it ever happened, yes or no?"

No one responded.

"Exactly. Professor Rogers is making things up as we go along to justify a position."

"Now, hold on—" Rogers said.

"I'm not done. You had your turn."

Ash gestured with his head for her to continue.

"Second, the split in the students' perceptions of Professor Kassimali is not, as Professor Rogers states, because of their political viewpoints. It is because of his failure—indeed, refusal—to allow the airing of contrary viewpoints in his classrooms. That is absolutely unacceptable. And that he might be an antisemite only further darkens the circumstances and raises a more serious question—whether he should be allowed to teach here at all."

"Get a grip, Susan," Professor Rogers said. "That sort of unhinged hyperbole is inappropriate. And let's not forget the other issue relative to academic curriculum. If Kassimali doesn't get tenure, his program goes bye-bye. It is identified with him. If he doesn't get tenure, he is gone and the program will fold up and close. We would be dealing a fatal blow to a thriving and essential part of the school curriculum, which, I might add, would likely have a ripple effect at other schools."

"More fundamentally, what will happen to the grants? Will the funding stream dry up?" Professor Rudman said.

A long pause.

"I think we are straying far afield," Rudman said into the silence. "We need to look at the criteria for tenure and see how they are weighted. The most important criteria are research and publications."

"That's an important point, Professor Rudman," Ash said.

"And let's not forget, the *potential* for both, especially research-based publications," Rogers said.

"*Potential?* Have you gone full-tilt looney, Rogers? Kassimali hasn't done *any* research, so his potential for doing research is an uninspiring zilch," Ash said.

"I think Abdullah Kassimali is an antisemite, and that should alarm all of us," Professor Klotz said.

"Antisemitism is a political opinion, and political persuasion is not a factor that we usually consider here, Professor Klotz," Rogers said.

"Antisemitism isn't a 'political opinion,' Rogers. It is unadulterated hate, pure and simple. But even if it were, collegiality is definitely an important factor in our decisions about tenure candidates," Susan Rothchild said, nodding at Klotz.

"If you don't mind me asking, Professor Klotz, are you Jewish?" Rogers said.

"I do mind you asking—and how is that an issue here?" Klotz said, raising her voice.

"Rogers, she's absolutely right," Ash said. "It's none of our business who is, or is not, Jewish, or anything else for that matter."

"I'm sorry," Rogers said, "but we should resist the instinct to inject our personal feelings into this process. The school and all affected rely on us to discharge our duties objectively, without bias, blind passion, or personal investment. Professor Kassimali has the freedom of speech to express his political opinion on Jews, and I dare say, we should not get involved with censoring colleagues. If you don't like what he has to say, don't listen. Change the damn channel. We already have set criteria for review. Professors' political opinions don't fall within our purview."

Ash rose with a burst of energy and went to grab another cookie. Rogers rolled his eyes and a few around the table smirked and shook their heads. The room went quiet as everyone waited for Ash to return to his seat. They knew the drill.

"Anyone else want to weigh in?" Ash said, exhaling loud enough for all to hear.

"Well, since we're talking about this sensitive topic, I'm concerned about that entire BDS movement. It has a violent agenda, Rogers, and should be booted from campus," Christian Rudman said.

"That's some serious fascist thinking, Rudman," Rogers said. "Are you a big fan of the committee regulating the faculty's political speech through tenure recommendations?"

Rudman stared at Rogers with narrowed eyes.

Rogers continued, "Here's the truth, as undesirable and painful as it might be for some of you. The university sanctions a wide berth of opinionated groups. That is—or *should* be—the hallmark of the school's free-speech culture. BDS is present on campuses across the country and beyond, and not a single school *in* ... *the* ... *world* has banned the BDS movement. Our campus boasts a rich collection of religious groups, political organizations, and social justice groups, and you want to pull a page from your Third Reich playbook and ban this one group? Perhaps you were Joseph Goebbels in a prior life? Or Genghis Khan? How about Joe McCarthy? Maybe the university should grant you the title of Minister of Political Correctness."

"Does anyone else have anything more to say? Megan? Bryce? Susan? Regan? Barbara? Anyone?" Ash said.

Heads shook around the table.

"Okay, let's take a final vote," Ash said, passing out a new batch of voting sheets.

"Connor, we assume you will vote this time. No more hiding behind the title, right?" Rogers said.

Ash flashed a big smile at Rogers but didn't respond.

When the voting sheets were returned to him, he tallied the results. "Okay, the vote is eight to three to deny tenure."

"Jesus," Rogers said. "I request that you poll each committee member to make sure everyone is locked in to their position."

"Professor Rogers, I admire your relentlessness, I do. But that is not happening. We are not jurors. We are professional colleagues." Ash flashed that same smile again and turned to Professor Singer. "Professor Singer, please prepare a full report for my review and delivery to the President."

Singer nodded.

"Ladies and gentlemen, thank you for your efforts and heartfelt expressions. We are adjourned."

In his heart of hearts, Ash felt the committee had done the right thing. They had come out on the side of principle and allegiance to governing standards. Knowing that, however, did not infuse him with satisfaction or relief. The road ahead promised turbulence and unforeseeable challenges. He kept returning to Rogers's comment about Joseph Goebbels. Even though it hadn't been directed at him, it had struck him like a lightning bolt. He was not sure why. He kept rewinding the meeting for a clue and found none. His chest tightened. The anxiety, drama, and tragedy of the past several days, combined with fitful sleep, filled him with an all-consuming weariness, like a severe case of jet lag. He craved a long, deep, and peaceful sleep, an escape to dream wonderland, under the protective cover of drifting, fluffy clouds and a reassuring, breezy sky. He doubted it would happen.

6

INCHING DARKLY INTO THE PAST

In the depth of the night, the clouds blocking the moon, Ash stole through a labyrinthine network of narrow, winding back streets and alleys that filled his nostrils with stale smoke and decay and his heart with fear and desperation. The buildings on both sides wore the scars of destruction—some gutted, some burnt, windows broken and blacked out, each building in abandoned dilapidation, beaten down by the course of history. The taller buildings blocked what sparse light still shone at that late hour from reaching the streets beyond, leaving Ash to move through corridors of darkness.

Head down, he navigated the streets with unwavering purpose, turning corner after corner on instinct, as if he'd taken the route many times before and was on his way to a familiar destination. He concentrated on minimizing noise and avoiding strewn debris, paying close attention to each step he took on the uneven, slick cobblestones. He eased each heel out first and then tenderly lowered the rest of the foot to the surface. His heart pounded against his chest in a steady rhythm like a pulsating bongo drum. Sweat collected on his brow and under his arms. Other than the occasional squeaking of his feet against the cobblestones, which each time caused his heart to miss a beat, not a sound could be heard.

Then he heard a slight squeal in the distance. Was it a cat? A rat? The screeching wheels of jeep? He paused for a tight second and then continued. He could not afford delay.

Then he heard it again, this time nearer. This time more human than not. He stopped and looked over his shoulder but detected nothing in the darkness, other than the sound of his own escalated breathing. A voice told him to retreat—whatever lay ahead was not his concern and he should return to his original location. Be smart. Be safe. Another voice urged him to proceed. He had to do what he had to do. Be brave. Be resolute.

When he turned the next corner, he noticed a dark figure halfway down the alley, illuminated by a sliver of moonlight that had managed to edge slightly beyond the cloud cover. From where he was, all that Ash could make out was that it was someone in uniform. Then he saw another figure, on the ground, rolled up like a silhouetted fetus, unmoving. And then a sound, not like the squeal from before, but the muffled cry of someone in pain and anguish. It was a woman.

Ash glanced behind him but found nothing there. He did not think the dark figure had seen him. Not yet, anyway. But continuing on could be the end of him—he shook inside with the revelation. He felt in his bones that whatever mission had landed him in this moment could implode with catastrophic consequences, well beyond whatever might be at stake in the alleyway in front of him.

Ash inched forward a few steps for a better look. What he saw froze him in his tracks. The dark figure wore a peaked cap with silver braid, affixed with the Nazi eagle-and-skull insignia. He was dressed in a thick, field-gray tunic that also brandished various insignia, including the same eagle and a swastika on the right breast. The uniform had a collar tab, indicating a rank that Ash could not make out from where he stood. But he knew the man standing there was a German officer, evidenced by the red armband with a white circle encasing yet another swastika, as well as the tapered breeches, which lined the insides of tall leather jackboots.

The Nazi officer was bent over, one hand behind his back, the other clutching the hair of the forlorn woman on the ground.

Without forethought, his eyes riveted on the scene before him, Ash took a few steps forward. He forgot to focus on the meticulous step-by-step technique he'd employed during his journey so far, and his feet squeaked on the slick cobblestones, a sound that echoed disproportionately in the narrow band of surrounding buildings and the all-consuming silence of the night.

Both the Nazi officer and the woman jerked their heads toward Ash. The Nazi's left hand released the woman and he straightened his back, revealing in his right hand a German spring baton.

"Come forward and identify yourself," the Nazi said. The voice was authoritative but calm and curious.

"No, run! Whoever you are, *run*," the woman said, her voice an anguished plea.

The familiarity of the voice took Ash off guard, and before the woman's words could register with him, the officer smacked her hard in the face with the back of his left hand, sending her sprawling to the cobblestones.

"Come forward," the officer repeated, louder this time, with an ominous tone and narrowed eyes. The officer took several steps toward Ash. They were now ten feet apart.

Ash slid to his right, toward the building nearest him, and positioned himself between both of them at a forty-five-degree angle. The Nazi smiled, a look of imminent conquest. Ash turned to the woman, who had lifted herself to one knee. The slice of moonlight through the hovering clouds glanced off her face. She was older, by maybe twenty or more years. *I know her*, thought Ash. *Who is she?* She looked at him with an imploring expression. For the first time, he noticed a narrow strip of blood down the right side of her face.

Ash repositioned himself, stepping carefully until he was squarely between the two of them.

"Run, please run," he said to the woman, waving his right hand down the alley.

She rose to her feet with effort but did not leave.

Ash slid closer to her now, firmly between her and the Nazi, his back to her, his eyes on him.

"Go... *please*," Ash said without turning to look at her.

The Nazi stepped toward Ash, close enough for him to notice the pungent odor of alcohol. The Nazi raised the baton at an angle over his shoulder and attacked Ash, who pivoted to his left and caught the blow on the underside of his raised left forearm. Pain shot through the arm and into his neck. He faltered but kept upright. The Nazi came at him again with the baton raised high in the air and brought it down toward Ash's head. Ash flung both arms in front and above him. The baton landed along his wrists, driving him to one knee. The Nazi raised the baton yet again, extending his arm outward for a sideways strike to the head. Before the baton hit its target, Ash thrust his shoulders forward into the Nazi's thighs and tackled him to the ground. The Nazi hit the ground hard, his head bouncing back into the cobblestones. Dazed, he dropped the baton, and it rolled a couple of feet away.

Ash turned to the woman. She had backed up several feet, still watching.

"*Go*, dammit! You must *go*," he said, rising from the ground, his left arm dangling.

The Nazi struggled to get back on his feet. Ash rushed to grab the baton as the scurrying of quick footsteps behind him grew fainter and fainter. The Nazi, still on the ground, grabbed and yanked his leg, upending Ash and sending him crashing to the ground. Ash rolled over, away from the Nazi, and managed to get on his feet. The Nazi started to rise, but before he could straighten, Ash kicked him in the face and sent him back to the ground, where he lay unconscious. Ash turned his eyes down the alleyway and saw an empty street.

Ash awoke drenched in sweat. He grabbed his phone off the nightstand. 3:30 a.m. He glanced at Caitlyn next to him in bed, sleeping like an angel. He sat up, breathing heavily, shoulders rising and falling, and reviewed the details of the nightmare. After fifteen minutes, he achieved ballast. Calm and clearheaded now, he nodded to himself. As counterintuitive as it was, and as much as he hated to admit it, Ashford Connor knew what he had to do once morning broke.

7

ROBERTSON REDUX

Ash had never set foot inside Cormac Robertson's home. He hadn't even spoken to the man since the conclusion of the investigation into President Uzinski's murder. Rumor had it that the Uzinski investigation had been the pinnacle of Robertson's distinguished law enforcement career, freeing his schedule to devote more time to his work with past-life regression. When Ash had learned about the career pivot, he'd rolled his eyes, shaken his head, and muttered, "Kumbaya." Truth be known, however, the incurably cynical Ash had conceded, if only to himself, that Robertson's past-life work with Caitlyn had born ripe fruit in solving the murder. In consequence, his curiosity had been piqued about its bona fides as an effective tool.

The morning after his nightmare, the moment the door shut behind Caitlyn on her way to teach her first class of the day, Ash called Robertson.

"We need to meet."

"About?"

"I'll tell you when we meet."

"Okay. When?"

"This morning, ten a.m.?"
"Sure. Where?"
"Your place."
"Good by me."
"And one more thing. No one can know about this meeting ... no exceptions."
"See you at ten."

To describe the route to Robertson's home as circuitous would have been a massive understatement. To get there required traversing a dizzying network of isolated and sometimes unmarked roads, with nary a sign of human existence, through an area several miles from campus that Ash had never known existed. The open entry gate, the left side bearing the letter C, the other R, introduced a long, uneven dirt driveway, the final destination masked. The house finally came into view when Ash reached the third bend in the road. Not another home could be seen in any direction.

Ash pulled up behind the pickup truck sitting in front of the garage of a two-story Victorian home, painted in olive green with black trim. Turning off the ignition, he laughed to himself and said, "Figures."

The Robertson residence did not square with what Ash had expected to see. The landscaping exuded attention and style, with an assortment of plants and flowers and colors you might find in a fairy tale. On entering, the first thing Ash noted was the built-in, floor-to-ceiling bookshelves that lined the walls of Robertson's living room, filled with an impressive collection of books—detective novels, true crime memoirs, historical fiction, mythology, Victorian-era fiction (including the complete works of Charles Dickens), forensic science textbooks, and books on psychology, psychiatry, life coaching, therapy, and counseling. A long, stately coffee table made of hand-carved, repurposed wood occupied the middle of the room. It had but one item on top: the seminal work *Many Masters, Many Lives*, by Brian L. Weiss, MD. Two identical French art deco leather armchairs, well-used, sat at a forty-five-degree angle to the coffee table, and a third sat several feet away, near a window that provided a long view of the hills and thick woods on one side of the home. There was neither a couch nor a television.

Ash declined Robertson's offer of coffee or tea but accepted his invitation to occupy one of the leather armchairs abutting the coffee table.

"So what brings you here, Professor Connor?"

"Can we dispense with the 'Professor' thing? Ashford or Ash will do fine."

Robertson smiled.

"I want to stress again that so far as the world is concerned, this meeting never happened."

"Okay."

Ash proceeded to share his personal history with his father, the childhood incident with his mother and his intervention, the dreams that followed, the contentious committee meeting about Kassimali's tenure candidacy, and the recent nightmare featuring a Nazi officer. He did not mention the Markowitz murder. The entire time, Robertson stayed mum and still, seemingly dialed in to every word.

When Ash had finished, he raised his eyebrows, as if pleading for a response. Robertson looked distracted, as if something had broken his concentration.

After a pregnant pause, Ash asked, "Well, what do you think this all means?"

"What do *you* think it means?"

"Dunno. I feel a vague sense of emptiness, like unfinished business."

"What about what's happening on campus?"

"Meaning?"

"Markowitz and Kassimali."

Ash leaned back. He scrolled to the recent nightmare with the Nazi in the alley.

"Ash, let's call it like it is. Your subconscious is trying to speak to you. How well do you want to listen?"

Ash looked away and pursed his lips. He wanted a cookie.

"Look, your head has danced around the edges of your past. Are you ready to take a deeper dive? It's the only way to figure this out."

Ash nodded to himself a few times, rocking back and forth. "How would that work?"

Robertson explained the hypnosis process. Once Ash was under, Robertson would probe him to gain insight into his past and cull information to help him understand what was happening.

"How's that sound to you?"

"Sounds fine."

"Questions?"

"Is this safe?"

"Safer than driving, and here you are."

Ash chuckled.

"Any other questions?"

Ash shook his head.

"Then close your eyes and lean back into the chair. Relax your shoulders and neck. Unclench your hands. Get super comfortable."

Robertson took Ash through an exercise designed to put him in a full state of relaxation, directing him to focus on three-dimensional breathing: first, inhaling through the nose, maximizing lung capacity by inflating his abdomen and rib cage and lengthening his spine; second, a short pause; and third, a long exhale through pursed lips, followed by a short pause. They repeated the exercise for eight minutes.

"Ash, keeping your eyes closed, I want you to envision a long stretch of white sand beach on a bright day, with a few scattered fluffy clouds and temperatures in the seventies. There is a slight, refreshing breeze coming off the sea. You are walking alone along the shoreline, the waves landing gently nearby and soothing your bare feet. It could not be a more perfect day. You will become the most relaxed you've ever been."

Robertson paused and allowed Ash to process. When Ash revealed a soft, almost-childish smile, Robertson renewed the breathing exercises. This time he had Ash hold his breath longer and exhale more deeply.

After several minutes of that, Robertson spoke. "Ash, listen carefully. Eyes still closed. When I say 'Go for it,' I want you to count down in your mind from ten to one. With each number of the countdown, you will become even more relaxed. Do you hear me?"

Ash nodded, ever so slowly.

"Go for it."

After ten seconds had passed, Robertson resumed. "You are in a tunnel on a train taking you to a part of your past, whirling through time. You will arrive during the 1940s in Nazi Germany . . . Are you there?"

"Yes."

"Are you alone?"

"Yes."

"How do you feel?"

"I'm nervous. Afraid."

"What are you wearing?"

"Dark clothes... drab, loose, worker clothes, and a cap pulled down over my eyes."

"How old are you?"

"Not sure... maybe eighteen or nineteen."

"Where specifically are you?"

"I'm in Berlin."

"What year?"

"1942."

"What are you doing?"

"I'm walking on cobblestoned back streets late at night."

"Why?"

"I, um... not sure... going somewhere I've been before."

"That's okay. Keep walking."

"What do you see as you walk?"

"Nothing. The streets are empty. There's no lighting save a thin sliver of moonlight penetrating the buildings."

"Are you close to your destination?"

"Yes, I've arrived. I'm at a door at an abandoned building. I knock five times... three quick knocks... a pause... two more knocks, the last one the loudest."

There was a lull in the session.

"What's happening, Ash?"

"Someone opened the door and escorted me down to the windowless basement. It's full of people milling about. A meeting is about to start."

"Who is meeting?"

"It's the Baum group."

"What is the Baum group?"

"It's an anti-Nazi resistance group that Herbert Baum formed. I'm the newest member of the group. We meet in secret to plan anti-Nazi strategies."

"Can you identify anyone at the meeting?"

"Yes. Several. Herbert Baum; his wife, Marianne Baum; Heinz Rotholz; Siegbert Rotholz; Hella Hirsch; Sala Kochmann; Suzi Baum; Stefan Heinrich."

"What is your name?"

"Chaim Hirsch, Hella Hirsch's younger brother."

"Does anyone look familiar to you?"

A long pause. "Hella Hirsch looks like a younger Caitlyn, and Herbert Baum resembles Bradley Markowitz."

"What is happening now?"

"The meeting has started. They were waiting for me. I was late for some reason."

"What is the meeting about?"

"Herbert is outlining our next strategy and reviewing each person's role."

"What is the strategy?"

"We're planning to use explosives to disrupt the Soviet Paradise."

"What is the Soviet Paradise?"

"A Nazi Party touring exhibition—propaganda designed to increase support for Germany's war against the USSR. It uses cartoons, photography, and movies to brainwash the public into thinking Jewish-Bolshevik control is at the root of all the problems the Soviet Union is having. It's a circus-like media campaign to fan the flames of antisemitism."

"What are the roles of the people in the meeting?"

"Marianne Baum will manage logistics and communications. Siegbert will reconnoiter the exhibition site. Sala will acquire the necessary materials to make bombs and assist in their construction. Heinz will be responsible for creating distractions at the event site to divert attention away from group members implementing the strategy. Hella is going to place and ignite the bombs. Suzi Baum will be a lookout. Stefan will coordinate the evacuation plan."

"What about you?"

"I am to assist my sister in placing the bombs."

"Do you say anything at the meeting?"

"Yes. I ask a question."

"What?"

"I ask our leader, Herbert, whether Joseph Goebbels will be there when we attack, whether he is a specific target."

"Why do you ask that?"

"I don't know."

"What does he say?"

"He says I should not be concerned with who will be there. I should only be concerned with the specifics of my job—any lack of focus and less than strict allegiance could prove fatal to everyone."

"When will the attack occur?"

"I-I-I'm not sure right now... I-I can't see or hear anything. I'm tired."

Robertson moved Ash with care into the present, first with breathing exercises and then a series of commands to put Ash in touch with his body: Wiggle your toes. Rotate your head and neck. Open and close your hands. He then directed Ash to open his eyes.

"How do you feel?"

Ash shook his head, as if trying to clear cobwebs. "I think I'd like that cup of coffee now."

"Not a problem."

"Would you also happen to have any chocolate chip cookies, by any chance?"

8

ASH AND THE TRIBE OF JUDAH

The session with Robertson rocked Ash in more ways than one. Fundamentally, it served up a personal epiphany of massive proportions, and not merely for what it potentially revealed about his historical roots. He'd had the sobering, if somewhat stunning, realization that for most of his life he had labored in self-delusion—he was not nearly the masterful intellect he'd fancied himself, nor was he the bright light those in the academic community had perceived him to be. His over-the-top personality, brashness, and signature charisma, he now recognized, were fragile masks for deep-seated insecurity and doubt. He had, with the aid of the iconoclastic Robertson, undergone a crash course in vulnerability and self-awareness.

As if that was not momentous enough, he now had to confront two life-altering potential realities: one, that past-life regression might not, after all, be spiritual mumbo jumbo or pseudoscience, but real and essential; and, two, that he might be a bona fide member of the Tribe of Judah. And there was one more thing. Both discoveries not only promised to redefine his existence, but embracing them would endow his wife with "I told you so" bragging rights. It would be, as he saw it, a rather juicy comeuppance.

But lest he get too far ahead with this monologue, Ash reminded himself that at bottom he was a man of science. He had staked his professional reputation on the sustaining and illuminating power of empirical data, in whatever form it took, and abhorred those who bathed their thinking and analysis in the subjective and instinctive. In his classroom, students tiptoed on thin ice any time they ventured near the speculative, especially when it came to understanding and learning the lessons of history. "What are the *facts*?" he often challenged. "Focus on the damn *facts*." Professor Connor had a mantra befitting his scientific mindset, which he called the ROPE: Be rational, be objective, be precise, and above all, be ethical. Anything less, he warned his students, would plummet them into the "quicksand of self-indulgence, the enemy of worthy discourse."

So when it came to his personal situation, before he could justify taking the leap into this new world order, Ash needed more facts—which, to this young professor, were lifeblood. Caitlyn had once commented that all families had "secrets," and family members did themselves a disservice by not uncovering and facing them head on. At the time he hadn't paid her any mind. She had also intimated that Ash might have Jewish blood flowing through his veins, a suggestion he'd shrugged off as one of Caitlyn's harebrained campaigns to bring him more in alignment with her. She had tried to tease his curiosity with a reference to her own past-life journey into Nazi Germany and her prior life at Auschwitz, claiming that she'd seen the "spitting image" of him there. A fascinating theory that had led Ash to mutter something under his breath about "Looney Tunes hour." Now, he wondered.

What do I not know about my family? Despite his natural skepticism, he felt a compelling desire to find out more, and he knew who would have answers.

He placed a call across the pond to Her Majesty's England.

"Hello, younger brother, to what do I owe the honor?"

"Brianna, I need to know something. I need the truth, and I mean the unvarnished truth."

"Oh-kay."

"I need to know about our heritage. I need to know if we're Jewish."

"Where's this coming from?"

"Never mind that for now. I need answers."

Brianna let out a long breath that echoed at the other end.

"Okay, Ash. So, yeah, we are Jewish... in part."

"Whose side of the family?"

"Dad's."

"Jesus. How can that be? We're Connors, from County Dublin, home of Oscar Wilde. Where's the Jewish in that?"

No answer.

"Brianna?"

"Okay, okay... Here's what I can tell you."

"I'm all ears."

"Dad fought in World War II. Captain Moses Elliot Abraham. 'Big Mo,' they called him. He was a pilot with the British Royal Air Force. As the stories go, he was dedicated to the cause and successfully flew many dangerous missions. But eventually the war took its toll on him. He was shot down over Dresden and rescued, but suffered severe burns. He struggled for months to survive, and later, when he was cleared to go home to England, he insisted on getting back to the action. One family member described him at that time as crazed, borderline maniacal.

"He made his way back to Allied lines and eventually hooked up with American soldiers liberating a Nazi concentration camp. He was so horrified by what he saw that he stayed with the American troops for several months to help the surviving prisoners. Allied forces and fellow Brit veterans referred to him as their 'Jew hero.' He didn't care. He was so single-minded.

"When he returned home to England, he was decorated with the Distinguished Flying Cross and Conspicuous Gallantry Cross, but by then he'd become a shell of himself and started drinking heavily. He wanted nothing to do with his military experience. He also didn't want the stigma of being Jewish—it was too painful for him—he wanted a new life. So he changed his name to Connor, in honor of one of his best buddies in secondary school who died in the war. He resettled in Great Britain, raised us in the Church of England, and never spoke to anyone about the war, our family history, or our Jewish roots. He wanted to erase it all—a totally clean slate—and everyone honored that."

Brianna exhaled and waited. The hum of the intercontinental phone line filled the silence between them.

"Ash, you there?"

"Um, yeah, yeah, I'm here. Listen, thanks. I gotta go. I'll call you again soon."

Caitlyn had once suggested that she and Ash take DNA tests and do a lineage search, confident the results would meet Ash's exacting scientific standards enough to alter his understanding of his roots. *No need now*, thought Ash. The dust on the new facts had not settled, but he saw the unmistakable writing on the wall. He couldn't—he wouldn't—deny his heritage anymore.

That did not mean he would become a "believer," like Caitlyn. Nor did it mean he would gravitate toward an emotional connection to Judaism or even any meaningful identity as a "Jewish" person. He had grown up Protestant. There was not a hint of Judaism in his background experiences. He also had nurtured a strong antipathy toward religion and notions of a higher power, regardless of religious affiliation. Yes, he was Jewish, technically speaking. He got that now. But that did not mean he had to excise his embedded values and moral code and replace them with something else. On the other hand, he was not, nor had he ever been, an antisemite. He respected the right of the Jewish people to practice their religion and observe their culture free from hatred and persecution, a view he had long held before this latest turn of events. Jews had their rightful place in the annals of humanity, which he would perpetually honor.

Socially, he was well situated. He could hold his own in any conversation that required a modicum of familiarity with Jewish history. He had read copious works about religious history, and Caitlyn had treated him to countless Bible stories over the years. The more pressing question was: Where would he go from here in terms of his relationship with Caitlyn and the trouble percolating on campus? He had some serious thinking to do.

Ash arrived home before Caitlyn and plopped his weary bones into the velvety, plush gray chair next to the bay window in the bedroom, where Caitlyn often sat to read. He scanned the room, admiring Caitlyn's discerning eye more than he ever had before. She had designed the bedroom to look like a suite at the Ritz-Carlton. Her Metropolitan taste—gold, stark white, and black lacquer—sprang to life in the Great Plains. Despite his rudimentary "artistic eye," Ash could appreciate the deftness with which she'd pulled the room together with an assortment of touches, selecting just the right paintings, rugs, lighting, color scheme, curtains, and furniture. The artistic meditations calmed him, a nice distraction to reset his emotional balance as he awaited the reckoning with his wife, allowing him to get better acquainted with his new reality.

He was warming to past-life regression. He was accepting his Jewish lineage. But with that item out of the way, there was still one thing, he knew, that would be a showstopper: a focus on God. He was, in Caitlyn's words, a God denier. The whole God thing made no sense to him. He viewed it as silly speculation, wishful thinking, an affront to science. Caitlyn, in contrast, was a rabid God believer and advocate.

That raised the unavoidable question: If he and Caitlyn stood at opposite pillars of the belief-nonbelief spectrum, how would they raise their children? Did their disparate perspectives threaten their union? Was there a middle ground acceptable to both? Would they teach religious concepts to the children? Would they instead educate the kids about their common moral concepts and life principles independent of religious affiliation? Would they foster mutual respect by openly discussing their different beliefs about the existence of God or a higher power? Would a top-down approach that favored one adult view over the other create a strained or even toxic environment? Or would they be better off with an open-ended approach, a pressure-free environment that encouraged the children to choose their own paths?

Maybe, Ash contemplated, he should accompany Caitlyn to the synagogue and experience a whole service. He could acknowledge that he'd never been willing to try to believe, or to engage in religious rituals. For the sake of his relationship, maybe he should give it a shot. What was the downside? He might differ with Caitlyn on the matter of God, but he respected her intelligence and admired her thoughtfulness. She came to her viewpoints with maturity and diligence. She did not operate out of fear or foolishness. Nor was she a maverick. Her main point, about which she was adamant, was that antisemites *had* to be God deniers; how could they believe in God and still hate the Jewish people— the very people God loves? For her, Judaism and God were two sides of the same coin.

Intellectually, she had a point. One could not have a reasonable conversation with extremists or Nazis about Jews. There, rationality did not have a chance. And perhaps that was how to come at this question of God. The individuals and groups that Caitlyn referred to as God deniers were unhinged and violent. These were not rational people, to say the least. Context mattered, and the context here was social justice, a space where Caitlyn excelled. From her perspective, Professor Kassimali's campus group, Peace in Palestine, embodied a grisly menagerie of protestors—violent, dangerous, explosive, and erratic. Some had targeted Caitlyn personally, and many had threatened Jews in emails and campus posters.

Ash could feel his mind expanding like a river thawing after a winter freeze. He tilted his body backward, gently placed his head on the back of the chair, and closed his eyes, his spirit softening. Soon afterward, though, his equanimity was disrupted by hurried footsteps hopping up the staircase.

"Ash, where are you? I have exciting news."

"The bedroom." Ash straightened up in the leisure chair.

Caitlyn rushed into their bedroom and sat down on their black, king-sized bed. "I found a past-life therapist for you." She seemed out of breath, not from the climb to the second floor but a thrill rushing through her bloodstream. "I've been researching past-life-regression therapists and found someone who will work with you virtually. Bryan Caldwell, in Colorado. I emailed him, and he responded that 'everyone has past-life memories.' This is the therapist for you, Ash!"

"I have a confession, Caitlyn."

"Oh."

"I'd planned to tell you soon, but now it's imperative."

"Uh-huh."

"Robertson and I had a past-life session the other day. I reached out to him—and swore him to secrecy—after I had a horrible dream where I found myself in Nazi Germany."

"Wow."

"Yeah, wow, exactly. He put me under, and according to him, I saw my earlier life as a late teenager working for an underground anti-Nazi group founded by Herbert Baum."

"Oh my God. I know all about the Baum group."

"And that's not all. You're gonna love this—I called Brianna and she fessed up. Our father was Jewish, a war hero. The war messed him up so badly, he not only became an alcoholic but changed the family name to Connor to create his version of the Iron Curtain between his past and present. My family name is Abraham. His first name—ready for this?—was Moses."

The blood drained from Caitlyn's face. She did not move a muscle, but her breathing quickened and her eyes widened. She stared at Ash, speechless. Then she shook her head a few times, the thoughts racing through her mind evident on her face.

"But here's the thing, my sweet. These new experiences—in all honesty, as important as they are—don't give me a belief in some higher power, some God. They stabilize me, increase my belief in myself. I mean, why do I need a God?"

"That's a fair question, Ash. But the problem as I see it is, you never connected emotionally as a child. It's hard for you to imagine any sort of spiritual relationship. Religion never meant anything to you. In fact, I'd venture that you rejected the idea of a loving God because of what you saw happen to your mom. You told yourself there couldn't be a loving God because of how she suffered. You empathized with her pain, and further, when your father abused her physically, he abused you emotionally. Does that make any sense?"

"Possibly. It's true that when he did those things, I felt it emotionally. I told Brianna that seeing him beat her was worse for me emotionally than if he'd beaten me instead. I couldn't stand seeing him whip her like that. I couldn't forgive him for beating our mom, but I could have forgiven him for beating me." Ash rubbed his face with both hands and let out a long, anguished groan.

"Ash, my love, I've told you before, it's more basic than that. You need to forgive yourself before you can move on emotionally. You need to forgive yourself for not protecting and saving your mother. Does that resonate in your heart and in your head? You're going to need time to process this. Don't expect a quick, dramatic change. It will be a gradual process."

"Look, let's face the facts, Caitlyn. I'm a nonbeliever. When you called me a God denier, it annoyed me, although

I suppose that's an appropriate designation. I've never believed in any aspect of religious life—no rituals, no traditions. I've always rejected God, and if I'm truly honest with you, I've ridiculed religious believers as fools. I've smugly justified my scientific work and scientific approach to life and living. I can't just shift gears intellectually or psychologically and start believing in some God because it's politically expedient."

"You need a personal experience that affects you emotionally. You can't feel differently about God because you've never really had a personal relationship with God. Does that make sense to you, Ash?"

"Not sure."

"The answer is a successful past-life-regression experience, and now you've had one. We should build on that. It's important to connect emotionally to formulate a belief system, and you just opened a door. There are likely other doors waiting for you to open."

"I hear you."

They rose and hugged each other.

"I'm in the mood for a chocolate chip cookie. Could you get me one? I'm too exhausted from all this discussion."

"Really?"

"Well, you know what I say. Chocolate chip cookies lie between sex and breathing!"

"Well, I'm not dragging my butt downstairs to get you a cookie. But perhaps you'd settle for joining me in this bed, and we'll see what we can do without the chocolate chips?"

9

THE NAVI SCHARF SEMINAR

Ash might not have come full circle to Caitlyn's worldview—he had a lifetime of resistance standing in the way—but his rapid-turnaround trust in Cormac Robertson and embrace of past-life regression stunned Caitlyn. In her wildest aspirations, she'd never imagined him landing there. When it came to past-life regression, she had considered him a lost cause. Once a past-life skeptic herself, Caitlyn Morrys knew the circuitous path to acceptance. It did not happen overnight. But knowing Ash as she did, knowing his fervent scientific mindset, not to mention his often-childish intransigence, she'd lacked even a shard of hope that he'd jump on board.

So when Ash disclosed that he'd reached out to Robertson on his own—when she absorbed that he was not toying with her, as he was wont to do—Caitlyn's imagination was fueled. What had happened with Ash represented the tip of the iceberg. Beneath the surface percolated something ominous, magnitudes larger than the two of them. Ash had opened a door to shed light onto his small world, and Caitlyn stood poised to rip the door off the hinges and invite the floodgates to enter.

She therefore placed a call.

"Hello, Professor Morrys. It's been a while. Let me guess. This is about your husband."

"You never disappoint, Inspector."

"What shall we talk about?"

"Ash told me about the regression session. Amazing. I'm still processing."

"Yes, understood. It was an astonishing breakthrough. He has, shall we say, some baggage."

"Well, don't we all... Look, I think he stumbled onto something much more profound than it appears on the surface. I want an audience with Dr. Navi Scharf. Can you make that happen?"

"Timing is everything. He has a conference coming up. Why don't the three of us attend and then visit with him privately?"

"You can do that?"

"Consider it done."

* * *

Caitlyn had attended a week-long Scharf seminar before and left a different person. Meeting fellow attendees and absorbing Scharf's lectures had recalibrated how she viewed not only herself and everyone in her life, but the world writ large. Her tipping point had been a specific group exercise. A seminar leader had two hundred people—an assortment of psychologists, social workers, therapists, and psychics from virtually every corner of the globe—pair off and form a circle en masse at the center of the banquet-sized room.

As people found partners and places to sit, Caitlyn felt a whoosh of energy coming her way and looked up to see an elderly woman bearing the name tag "Bonita" approaching, gray eyes sparkling. She stood five feet, if that, had a silver-gray bun at the back of her head, a pencil stuck over her ear, and a pair of glasses on a beaded gold chain hanging around her wrinkled neck. She sat to Caitlyn's right, smiled a warm, seductive smile, and squeezed Caitlyn's arm like she was a long-lost sister.

"Hello," she said, in a thick accent that betrayed a Spanish upbringing. "Is this the first time for you?"

"Yes. I've never done this before. I'm not going to be good at it."

"Let's first exchange our glasses. I will hold yours and you mine."

They made the exchange.

"Now, holding my glasses, close your eyes, relax your shoulders, empty your chest of air, and tell me what you see."

Caitlyn obeyed but saw nothing other than the darkness of her inner eyelids. She opened her eyes, shook her head, and turned toward Bonita. "I guess I just don't believe in all this."

"You're resisting, you're working against yourself." Bonita closed her eyes, squinting tightly, and held Caitlyn's glasses out at arm's length, disappearing into a galaxy of thought.

Several seconds later, Bonita began speaking. "I see a man. A proud and handsome man. He is at a funeral in England. A family is present, a sister and mother. The man is stoic, almost distant, not crying. Maybe conflicted. He has a look of someone who wants to leave. Does this mean anything to you?"

Caitlyn inhaled and exhaled, mouth closed, and softly nodded, her gaze darting around to catch glimpses of what others might be doing.

"You still doubt me," Bonita said. "I can see it in your face. The funeral was for the patriarch of the family. There was bad blood."

Caitlyn's eyes widened and she turned toward Bonita. She started to speak and stopped.

Bonita took her glasses from Caitlyn and handed Caitlyn's back to her. She stood and patted Caitlyn on the shoulder.

Caitlyn raised her eyes to meet Bonita's. She froze. Her chest tightened and she averted her eyes.

"We all start out as skeptics. It is the natural point of departure. It is where Dr. Scharf started. Understand that. You are no different than the rest of us. We professionals spend our entire adult lives relying upon evidence-based methods to learn truths. We prioritize scientific data. We thrive on it. Depend on it. But we owe the world an obligation to remain curious, to ask questions, and to recognize what we cannot explain away with scientific methods. Science functions only with an open mind, and in the end, we are on a shared quest to find ways to heal and improve our collective existence. Think about that."

Before Caitlyn could respond, Bonita disappeared in a flash, like a flame snuffed out by a strong wind.

A chill crept up Caitlyn's back. She had come to the view, long before the seminar, that there were no coincidences in the universe. All that happened had a purpose, and humanity existed and persisted under the gaze of an underlying order of intelligence. Serendipity was not a species of luck. It was not random. It was a force guiding people along their life paths. And she was smart enough to know that taking the leap from that perspective to a belief in past-life regression was not that tall an order—in theory. But still she resisted. It was one thing, she reasoned, to see what occurred in your life as part of an overall scheme that transcended each individual. It was another, a fundamentally different other, to expand that mindset to accept existences long since past, beings that could only be seen, felt, and touched in the deep subconscious.

Until that episode with Bonita, Caitlyn had reduced the possibility of past lives to a cosmic puzzle beyond the comprehension of the logical human mind, best deposited inside a box full of other interminable conundrums, useful for social party banter but nothing more. But sitting there at the seminar, alone, the entire room of people now a blurry background, a powerful yearning to embrace what Bonita had told her erupted within, ratcheting her heartbeat up. And rather than resist out of some ingrained skepticism, as Ash would do, she wanted to succumb. She wanted to believe.

Her own epiphany had arrived while working with Robertson to help solve the murder of President Uzinski and avert her own execution. The results could not be denied—the parallels were too spot-on to brush away as odd coincidences. Now, Ash—miracle of miracles—had climbed on board. Caitlyn knew they were on the cusp of something powerful.

* * *

True to his word, Robertson had set up a private meeting with Dr. Scharf following his keynote address at the conference. As a lecturer, Dr. Scharf did not disappoint. He explored the symbiotic relationship between present traumas and unresolved issues from past lives. Using examples from his clinical work, he demonstrated how regression models uncover and confront lingering problems and provide solutions—or, at a minimum, clarity. He highlighted how we "reunite, lifetime after lifetime, with people we love, and there's no such thing as death." He peppered his talk with provocative illustrations that kept the audience spellbound.

The talk, however, engendered palpable unease in some quarters. In Caitlyn, it triggered disquiet over the daunting prospect of meeting up again with people she hated, people she'd prefer had never existed, as had happened during the Uzinski murder investigation and the past-life-regression sessions she had undertaken with Robertson. Sitting in the audience, she wondered whether her experiences were typical. Were they merely isolated events within the narrow parameters of her individual life? Or did they foreshadow more pervasive patterns that repeated on a large scale? What were the implications for modern times that sadistic Germans had massacred six million people in the daylight of a knowing world that had turned collective blind eyes to the horror? It took a lot of people to murder six million people. It took more—many, many more—to let it happen with appalling complacence. What had happened to all their souls, whether murderers, accessories, or spineless bystanders? Where were their souls now? What kinds of people did they occupy? The prospects frightened Caitlyn.

Once the keynote was over, Robertson ushered Ash and Caitlyn into a private meeting room where Dr. Navi Scharf awaited them. After pleasantries and introductions, they got down to business.

"We are grateful to have this private time with you," Caitlyn said.

"Not at all," Scharf replied. "Inspector Robertson told me about the turmoil on the Coronado campus. How can I help?"

"We have, I believe, a potential connection between what is happening on campus now and past-life relationships," Caitlyn said. "The campus is burning with political controversy. It's a divisive and combustible situation. People crave a solution, and, of course, not everyone is on the same page. We've been wondering whether prior alliances might be implicated—maybe old alliances have been renewed, and some don't realize they exist and need to find their way back to each other."

"That," Scharf said, "is a powerful insight, Professor Morrys. Political movements, much like personal relationships, can carry over from past lives. People often reincarnate into similar roles with shared goals. When individuals feel an intense pull toward a political cause, especially when they find themselves in the midst of others who share that sense of purpose, it can be a continuation of a mission from a previous incarnation."

"I have this strong feeling, almost a certainty," Caitlyn said, "that we've fought these battles before—with the same comrades. It's like... when you meet someone for the first time, but you feel like you've been fighting alongside them for centuries. Could it be that in a past life, we were part of the same political movement or revolution?"

Scharf leaned forward in his seat. "Many souls carry a sense of purpose that transcends lifetimes. For some, that purpose is personal. For others, it's societal or political. If you think about social movements, or even political upheavals, throughout history, they are not random events. Passionate individuals are their driving force—souls who have toiled tirelessly for the same or similar causes for decades upon decades. When they reincarnate, they gravitate—maybe not right away, but at some point—toward similar issues and, in the process, find each other. What seems happenstance is the natural order of things."

Ash interjected, "May I say something here?"

All eyes turned to Ash, and Scharf nodded expectantly.

"I'm new to this, and honestly, I'm still wrapping my head around the basic idea. But I want to be clear about what you're saying. Are you saying that people who are brought together for a cause today—specific people—might have been comrades in past lives, even centuries ago?"

"That is what I am saying," Scharf said. "It is not certain, but it is a distinct possibility. Understand that when souls are emboldened to create change, the power of their energy transcends their corporeal beings and continues to land somewhere across time barriers. It is not their minds. It is their spiritual essence, the ultimate search engine."

Ash dropped his gaze and nodded to himself, processing.

"Let me give you a precise example. Say you have a friend who is passionately involved in environmental activism in this life, but in her regression sessions identifies herself as a member of a marginalized group of indigenous healers who, centuries ago, fought to protect the land from colonizers. The parallels are too uncanny to ignore. In essence, she is continuing a battle she undertook a long time ago."

"Is that a hypothetical?" Ash asked.

"No, Professor. That is a client of mine. According to Dr. Brian Weiss, a soul's purpose doesn't change because the body gives out. And the kind of energy you are talking about here has a magnetic and vibrant quality. It is restless. It is driven. It needs to find a place to operate."

"Dr. Scharf, I mean no disrespect when I ask you this," Ash said, his brow furrowed. "I'm just curious. How is the soul to which you refer different than, say, what Catholicism or Protestantism says about souls?"

"That, Professor Connor, is an excellent and vital question. In past-life regression, Dr. Weiss describes the soul essentially through a therapeutic lens. It is a vehicle for spiritual growth that carries forward experiences, memories, pain, and suffering. It transcends space and time. In more traditional religious circles, like Catholicism or Protestantism, the soul emphasizes a singular, unique life that has no repeat performance. It is a onetime journey that records merit or sin with a determined external outcome. A one and done, you might say. In that sense, it's the antithesis of what we refer to as reincarnation."

"And so you reject the notion of the Catholic or Protestant soul?" Ash asked.

"I would not put it that way," Scharf said. "Both are mysterious ways of looking at existence and have a common thread: the search for growth, love, forgiveness, and redemption. The goals, ultimately, converge. The timelines over which those goals can be met differ. From our perspective, certainly mine, the soul is engaged in a virtually perpetual search for completion, no matter what vessels they occupy, good or evil, over the course of a series of lives. The soul continues to search until it finds love and healing. The basic quest and values are similar. I don't think, in the end, the differences are that significant."

Caitlyn said, "I take it, Dr. Scharf, that the endless journey of the soul applies to political figures, like everyone else? The souls of leaders of yore are tracked to fill the shoes of today's leaders?"

"Yes, quite possible—in fact, likely. Think of heartfelt passionate social or political missions as having a continuum that transcends life as we tend to experience it."

"And that, presumably," Ash said, "applies to the personal bonds once formed. They're not merely personal bonds, they're bonds of the soul, yes?"

"Well said," Scharf said with a smile.

Caitlyn grimaced. "What about the negative part of the equation? What about souls that have bad unfinished business, like someone like Hitler or Goebbels?"

"Sadly, yes," Scharf said. "The universe is not an arbitrator of what souls get to reincarnate. This process is nondiscriminatory."

At this last comment, the energy around the room dipped.

Scharf continued, "Keep in mind that the souls we encounter, whether they're our allies or adversaries, are part of our spiritual journey. That does not mean that souls can't evolve and grow. It does happen. But the sources are deep and extensive."

"So," Ash said slowly, "even our fiercest political battles have a spiritual dimension. They're not just about the issues at hand—they're part of a much larger, soul-driven process."

"Yes. You got it. I would add this, however. Modern struggles in the arenas of inequality, freedom, and justice echo past lifetimes where the same issues were at play. The soul seeks balance, harmony, and evolution, and often that happens through political and social engagement."

A long silence ensued. Ash leaned back in his seat and exhaled. Robertson caught his eye and Ash nodded.

Scharf finally spoke into the quiet. "Appreciate this as you go forth. The soul is eternal and transcends the confines of any particular lifetime. The body, on the other hand, is temporary, committed to a specific time and place. In successive lifetimes, the soul occupies a new vessel. It can be man, woman, or child and harbors no preference in terms of occupation and personality. It merely has unfinished business, a continuous thread over time. Once you accept that, the possibilities are virtually endless."

Robertson rose and extended his hand. "Dr. Scharf, we are most grateful for your time and insights. Hugely helpful."

"Glad to be of help. Best of luck to you."

10

THE MARKOWITZ LETTER

During the trip home from the conference, Ash and Caitlyn left each other to their own thoughts. But Ash could tell, beyond a glimmer of a doubt, that Caitlyn was champing at the bit to concoct ways to marshal the troops and rouse consciousness in response to the storms swirling on campus. Each time he stole a glance in her direction, he saw in her eyes a parade of thoughts and strategies, like an assembly line churning out product.

Before the Markowitz tragedy, Caitlyn had eased into the deep background of the public stage, a deliberate retreat that lifted the shadow she'd cast over Ash and allowed him to carve out a distinct public persona. He'd be the first to admit he enjoyed the broadened limelight, savored it, even, and the last to admit he did not like—and sometimes resented—playing second fiddle to the ubiquitously admired Caitlyn. She possessed something he never had—instant likability—while he sported a chip on his shoulder that could unbalance people unless and until his sheer intelligence and boyish charm won them over.

But while her earlier decision to take a back seat had liberated him from the constraints of her larger-than-life image, her popularity on campus had not waned. On the contrary, the recent events, which had resulted in a rush of students in acute need of counseling, had intensified her magnetic power. Her return to the spotlight would be seamless, and the meeting with Dr. Scharf left little question that she was about to retake center stage. Ash could read the tea leaves—he feared that, while Caitlyn began to steadily pivot to a renewed role in campus politics, his recent ascension to campus leadership might be short-lived.

The larger question, in his mind, at least, was where his future might be headed. While he'd never told anyone, he'd long coveted the role of university president, especially after Caitlyn made clear, in response to countless overtures and expressions of support, that she had no interest in what many viewed as her destiny. In fact, in most professional circles on campus, after the criminal investigation into the Uzinski murder had ended, it was assumed she would be the next school president. Once she'd defused the widespread expectations, some colleagues had encouraged Ash in that direction. It never failed to tickle his ego, but he'd downplayed and shrugged it off. *Play it close to the vest*, he kept telling himself. *Don't obsess about it. Let it happen organically.* And so, he'd put the aspiration on the back burner of his mind. It was not until now, as he contemplated the unnerving prospects of losing his upward career trajectory, that it struck him how much he wanted the job—and the title.

What would become of him if his career bottomed out? Was his fate to teach the same classes every year and suffer the monotonous sound of his voice peddling the same lectures and tired phrases and jokes until he got the unceremonious boot of forced retirement? Maybe he'd be better off leaving Coronado and replanting elsewhere. A proverbial fresh start to reinvent himself.

That tantalizing thought—leave the university and all its political baggage—in turn produced another, more ominous one: Did he really want to raise a family now, as he and Caitlyn had discussed? The idea of a family freaked him out. Had they gotten ahead of themselves? In light of recent events, should they see how things shook out before taking any bold steps? For the first time since he'd been with Caitlyn, he questioned his commitment to raising a family. And for the first time since gaining professional notoriety, he had become emotionally unmoored.

Those were his thoughts, a stream of uncertainty flooding his system and massive self-doubt percolating in his psyche, as they arrived home. By then, Ash knew that Caitlyn would no longer be content to keep her internal musings to herself, and he would be forced to cast aside his depressing monologue. Sure enough, after they settled in for the evening, Caitlyn wanted to get into it.

"Ash, sweetie, we're on the verge of something huge."

"Which huge? It would appear we've lately cornered the market on huge."

"What we learned from Dr. Scharf about how groups are connected in past lives."

"Is that how we find Markowitz's killer?"

"That's not our problem. You saw the campus. It's crawling with law enforcement interviewing students and faculty and sectioning off campus spaces for a widespread investigation. They've got it handled."

"From your lips to God's ears."

"We've got bigger fish to fry. Can we focus on that?"

Ash squinched his brow and eyes, his stock expression of skepticism, but leaned back and clasped his hands in his lap.

"In the past several days, as the primary academic advisor and counselor for the Psychology Department, I've spoken with more students than I can count about safety and campus security—almost all Jewish students. They're distraught, to say the least."

"Okay."

"I've even fielded calls from parents."

"Ah, yes, the entitled world we live in."

"That's unfair, Ash. They're worried, and they have reason to be. You would be, too, if it were your child. Something you'll better appreciate soon enough."

Ash winced.

"Parents are threatening to pull their kids from the school. Think about a half-filled classroom during your popular lectures."

"I'm kinda warming to that prospect."

"What is wrong with you?"

"Nothing is wrong with me. Why?"

"Your attitude leaves much to be desired."

He shrugged.

"The day before we left for the Scharf conference, I had fifty-two messages—*fifty-two*—from agitated parents. When do you recall that ever happening?"

Ash stayed quiet.

"Every student who met with me bashed Kassimali, labeled him an unabashed antisemite. They complained about how he puts Israel down in his classes, and they blame him—perhaps not directly, but morally—for what happened to Markowitz. Some even said he brought outsiders to the rally from Antifa, those violent, fanatical extremists. There's a groundswell of energy, a coming together. It's palpable... and ominous."

"Okay, Caitlyn, slow down a second. May I make an observation?"

She stared at him with eyes wide open, bestowing grudging permission to speak.

"I know you care about these students. And I accept they are distraught. But therein lies the problem. You're getting your ears filled with a regurgitated, one-sided perspective from a deeply biased group. It's like listening to a Fox News program, a group of disgruntled students who can't see straight—"

"That is not—"

"Let me finish, please. You're an advisor to them, a talented one, I might add, with expertise in clinical psychology. You're the quintessential great listener. You care about your students, more than most, way more than most. You're ideally suited to help them adapt and feel safe. In that lane, you're the best. You are not, however, conducting an investigation, running a political campaign, or organizing a revolution. There are other points of view, some doubtless held by people who believe in fundamentally different facts than what you are hearing. People are bordering on the unhinged. Hysteria is the last thing we want to foster. After all, we are—or purport to be—a citadel of free speech. Help your students get better, nurture them, but don't ride with them on high horses into blurry battlefields."

"Look, I realize our wonderful President Brightson has done a less-than-stellar job of navigating between political correctness and free speech—the boundaries keep changing. We've got two conflicting mantras on campus, and that's contributed to this nightmarish situation and the violence.

But we can't sit idle here. We have leadership responsibilities, and we're well suited for the task."

"Be careful. We have a thriving Islamic studies program and cultural center. It's nationally distinguished. Those interested in that course of study are entitled to learn and to have a platform. And much as you—or I, for that matter—might not like it, Professor Kassimali is entitled to a platform and to teach in the manner he thinks best. And let's not be blind to the reality that his program generates millions of dollars annually in grant money and donations. It's not necessarily us versus them."

"Speaking of whom, I intend to talk to President Brightson about Kassimali's tenure application. I want to reaffirm the UPC's recommendation to deny him tenure."

"Why do that, Caitlyn?"

"Why not? I've earned the prerogative, haven't I? I have experience in the matter of tenure, lest you forget."

"What prerogative? You're no longer on the UPC. It's no longer part of your charge. The UPC, as currently constituted, has it well in hand."

"Are you trying to suppress *my* speech?"

"You're missing the point. Having an opinion does not entitle you to inject yourself into an official process that no longer includes you. Besides, there's another reason you'd be well-advised to tread softly. It would be no small irony for you to seek to drown out a controversial voice while at the same time mouthing platitudes about the vital importance of academic tenure—as an unofficial gatecrasher, no less. Remember what you once said when you sat in the chair: 'Academic tenure is the strong foundation for American freedom and democracy.'"

"I see nothing wrong with an off-the-record chat with the President of the school where I teach and enjoy standing and possess extensive institutional memory."

"Be forewarned."

"Let's go back to our discussion with Scharf and what it might mean. You remember Josh?"

"Yeah, one of your student pets."

Caitlyn glared at Ash. "As you know, Josh is a bright light at this school. A potential valedictorian. The kind of student who will make a notable mark in life, become a coveted alum, make us all proud, even the cynical Ashford Connor. He's thoughtful and, I might add, *mature*, which we can use a little more of."

"What's your point?"

"He came to see me... all beside himself. He witnessed the murder. He complained incessantly about Professor Kassimali and said he can't see staying at an institution that tolerates antisemitism. He's considering a transfer to NYU. His parents have insisted he do so."

"Whadja tell him?"

"Pretty much what I just said about his stature and importance here, how essential he was to the betterment of the institution."

"How did he receive that?"

"Well, humbly. But more than that—he talked about a solution."

"Oh? What?"

"Josh suggested we hold a series of student-only meetings to address the venom on campus. There's a group of students who have gravitated to each other, who seem to have a special bond, or as Josh put it, 'a resistance connection.' He volunteered to help run those meetings and wanted me directly involved. It was as if he had eavesdropped on our meeting with Scharf. He may not know what he's on to, but I do, and I want to make it happen."

Before Ash could respond, they heard a hard, authoritative knock on the front door.

"We expecting someone, Caitlyn?"

"Nope."

Ash glanced at the clock, rose, and went to the door.

"Inspector Robertson... what... why—"

"May I come in?"

"Sure... please."

Robertson removed his aviator glasses and hooked them into his shirt, a sure sign that a serious conversation was impending. After the three adjourned to the living room, Robertson slid a sealed letter out of his pocket and handed it to Caitlyn.

"Read it out loud, please."

Caitlyn opened the envelope and unfolded the letter.

"Dear Professor Morrys," she read, then looked up at both men. "If you are reading this letter, I am dead and most probably"—she gulped and shot glances at each of them in turn—"I have been killed at the rally later this afternoon by someone doubtless incited by Professor Abdullah Kassimali. I predicted that this would happen at some point, and that when it did, it would set off a sequence of events that will hopefully change the course of world history. Remember always, I am merely a messenger in this life. And now, I am happy to say, my work is done. Your work with your daughter, Rebecca, however, is just beginning. May Hashem, the Name of the One, guide you and protect Rebecca so she may fulfill her mission in this lifetime on earth—to ready the world for the coming of the Moshiach, the Anointed One. Sincerely, Bradley Markowitz."

Caitlyn's face had drained of color. "How did he know I was pregnant? How did he know I was having a girl? How did he know her name was going to be Rebecca?"

"What the hell are you talking about?" Ash said, a rush of anger rapidly rising from his chest to his head.

Caitlyn started sobbing softly.

"Are you pregnant?"

"Yes, I was going to tell you soon."

"Soon! But rather than tell me, you concocted a scheme to have a messenger announce the happy event through the voice of a dead man. How delightfully theatrical of you. And the Academy Award goes to . . . the heartless and selfish Caitlyn Morrys!"

Ash turned to Robertson. "And you, *Inspector*, he of the sanctimonious moral code, explain yourself."

Caught off guard, Robertson blushed and his face froze. He looked at Caitlyn and back at Ash. "I . . . uh . . . I, um . . . didn't know. I assumed—"

"You *assumed*? You assumed that if my wife was ripe with child, surely her devoted and loyal husband would be aware of that trifling nugget of information. *But of course.* Let me be the first to congratulate you on your uncanny powers of deduction."

"Ash, please—"

"Ash, please, my ass. Spare me the mumbo jumbo. I want to know what's going on here, and I want to know now."

After a few seconds of silence, Robertson stepped into the breach. "Look, Ash, I didn't know about the pregnancy. But in terms of the rest of the letter, it says what it says. I suggest you leave it for future consideration. Markowitz obviously perceived that your daughter will be endowed with a special mission in her lifetime, and only she can tell you what that is. That's the gist, as I see it." He stood. "I think it best I leave."

"Sounds like an excellent plan, Inspector," Ash said, all the while glaring at Caitlyn, who had her head down.

After Robertson had left, Ash pushed his long hair back behind his ears and stared at Caitlyn. "Here's what's going to happen. I'm going to take a shower, and when I am finished, I'm returning to this room. And when I return, if you want this marriage to survive the night, you will have gathered your thoughts and assembled a Hall of Fame explanation for why I am learning now and in this way that, one, you are pregnant; two, you know it's a girl; and three, you somehow thought you could name our child without my input. Once we have your no-bullshit explanation, we can take stock of our life together."

He turned and marched upstairs, each step in deliberate cadence, echoing in the home.

When he returned twenty minutes later, Caitlyn had not budged from where she'd first sat down.

"Ash, okay. I screwed up. I admit it. I don't know what came over me. I didn't—"

"You knew you were pregnant when we were at the conference?"

"Yes."

"Unreal."

"How long had you known?"

"About ten days."

"Jesus... and when did you learn the gender?"

"Same day. Look, in hindsight, I screwed up. But understand, I didn't want to distract you with all you had on your plate. You were under tons of pressure. The Markowitz talk was a major happening. I didn't think a few days mattered."

Ash shook his head a few times. "Do I even know who you are?"

Caitlyn began to cry again.

"You have humiliated me."

"I understand totally. I am so, so sorry."

"And what is with this mission idea? How can my daughter have a life mission before she has a life? What are you all thinking?"

"I don't think Robertson or anyone else knows that. And I don't know—and I don't think Robertson knows—if Rebecca is a new soul or if she's had a past lifetime. But I think she will be special and will have a message to deliver."

"Message? What message? Earth to Caitlyn. Tune in, please. Make some sense. I can't deal in these cryptic clues about old souls traveling together and their life missions. It's our child we're talking about. And where did that name even come from? She's not even here yet! Is this conversation actually happening? Are we in a past life?"

"Rebecca is a biblical name. My favorite. I believe Rebecca is being sent here to deliver a message from God, in *our* lifetime, to *our* world."

Ash looked at Caitlyn as if she'd gone mad.

"Think, my love," Caitlyn said in an imploring tone. "What if Robertson is right? Just hear me out. What if Rebecca isn't a typical child? What if she knows, as a child, that she's had a past life? Are you going to tell her she's wrong? That the poor thing is just having bad dreams? Will you try and dissuade her? Ash, are you going to tell Rebecca she's crazy?"

Ash was watching her now as he might an actor on stage, playing the role of someone who had gone off the deep end.

"We need to think this through. I'm afraid, Ash. I'm afraid for our child. I don't want her labeled crazy, or sick, or psychotic. We need to figure out what to say to her and how much to question her about all of this. Don't you agree?"

"Agree? The only agreement that comes to mind is agreeing that you're nuts. I mean, do you hear yourself? You're pregnant with our child—it *is* our child, is it not?—and you're rambling about whether she might be psychotic. She hasn't even graced our presence, for crying out loud."

Ash shook his head again several times.

Caitlyn bowed her head and exhaled deeply, her shoulders dropping.

"Enough. I'm praying that in the morning this will all have been a bizarre dream and you will have returned to your senses."

"Ash, please don't run away emotionally. Rebecca and I both need—"

"Stop. Enough of this craziness. Just stop."

Ash walked upstairs to the bedroom, shaking his head continuously and muttering under his breath. The bedroom door clicked closed, barely audible downstairs. Caitlyn rose and shuffled into the kitchen to start up the Jura machine. She needed a flat white coffee.

Behind the closed door upstairs, out of earshot, Ash held his head in his hands and sobbed, which he had not done since the days when his father had beaten his mother.

11

GAME PLAN RISING

After two days of tiptoeing around each other in polite distance, elephants in the room left unattended, the mood in the Morrys–Connor household returned to near normal. Ash had had ample time to decompress and reconfigure and return to the land of the rational, where he operated best. His wife, while doubtless champing at the bit to engage him in serious political matters, had given him the space and time to regain his ballast—a gift he treasured. And he'd gotten over Caitlyn's poor judgment regarding the pregnancy news. They could revisit that gleeful subject soon enough. For the time being, roaring on the front burner were issues regarding the state of life on the Coronado campus. He resolved to allow her to break the ice.

That morning, before making their respective ways to campus for routine duties, they gathered in the kitchen. She sat at the table, a cup of flat white coffee in front of her, while he remained standing, cup of tea in hand, leaning against the counter.

"Ash?"

"Uh-huh?"

"I need your help."

"Okay."

"I'm struggling with what we heard from Navi Scharf. I can't get my head around what seem like contradictions or at least concepts that my little brain can't fathom."

Ash knew the display of vulnerability was not spontaneous. Caitlyn knew how to bring him into the center of things, and he was a sucker when she did. He didn't mind. It made him feel needed and included while playing to the strength of his considerable intellect. It was how their codependency often worked.

"The meeting confused you?"

"Not exactly. I've been trying to reconcile what he told us during the meeting with comments he made during the lecture. It's wracking my brain."

"Reconcile? How do you mean?"

"How do you explain the past-life-regression theory of love and redemption in light of all the hate and evil? Taking Brian Weiss at face value, how do you reconcile all the horribles around us, on campus and in the world, with God's plan for the steady evolution and growth of humans across generations of past lives?" She opened her arms wide.

"That's the world we live in. God couldn't care less about what happens, because God doesn't exist. God is a figment of the imagination. We're a screwed-up race of beings. We've been maiming, killing, raping, and plundering more than we've been enjoying sunsets, or each other, or chocolate chip cookies. Those are not contradictions. They're business as usual for the human race. It's who we are."

"And there, ladies and gentlemen, is the quintessential Professor Ashford Connor, the ultimate fatalist." She took a deep breath. "Ash, I don't think that's what Dr. Weiss is getting at. He advances a model of love and the progressive evolution of all souls—a constant expansion toward the unity of souls and oneness with God. He paints a rosier picture than your Chicken Little 'sky is falling' mindset. The part I don't understand is, how do you explain thousands of years of systemic antisemitism along the growth continuum? If our souls are becoming progressively more loving and God-like, why hasn't the hatred filtered out across generations of past lives and renewed souls? Suspend your innate skepticism for a moment. How does that make any sense?"

"Look. No disrespect, but the more we talk about this, the more it sounds like kooky talk again, like it did when you first began to dabble in past-life regression with Inspector Robertson."

"Ash—"

"No, wait. I don't mean to be difficult or cute. I'm serious. Maybe this time, rather than seeing the light, as I thought I did, I got caught up in the emotional angst of childhood issues. I needed something to break, some sort of infusion of new energy to rebalance me. Maybe I projected more into it than was, in fact, there. It happens. So now your confusion is making me doubt what we're even doing here."

She dropped her eyes and he sipped his tea.

"But let's take your premise at face value. How would you rationally test whether what you perceive as opposites or internal contradictions can be reconciled?"

"Well, first, I don't see rationality as the yardstick. This isn't science."

"Okay."

"I'm thinking we need to go to the source and collect a different kind of data." She opened her eyes wide, tempting his interest.

Ash choked on his tea. "You're kidding, right? You want to collect data from souls?"

"Ash, please. We could regress patients under hypnosis to determine where their souls are located along an evolutionary continuum. That doesn't sound like much of a leap to me. The premise is, the more past lives they've had, the further they are on the journey toward God."

He shot her a look that blended curiosity with concern for her mental well-being. "Caitlyn, after my session with Robertson, I did some research."

"More quintessential Ashford Connor."

"Thank you. And I learned about hypnotic suggestibility. Heard of it?"

"Ah-ha."

"I began to wonder about what happened with Robertson and me. Because of his work with you, maybe he had a jaundiced view of how it should be with me. Somehow, intentionally or not, he got me to see things in my past that are spiritual false flags, if you get my drift."

She squinched her face, disappointed, and shook her head. "Now we have Ashford Connor, the quintessential *skeptic*. You've got to trust the process or you don't play."

"Gathering data from strangers under hypnosis?"

"Well, maybe not strangers. We identify those similarly struggling with what's happening on campus, as I alluded to when we met with Scharf."

"You're perfectly serious about this, aren't you?"

She looked into his large, soulful eyes. "I don't know how else to explain how antisemitism has continued to flourish so perniciously for thousands of years. People aren't learning. People aren't changing. Why? Where is the progressive awakening? What are the patterns? What are the indications?"

"What do you mean, specifically?"

"Take, for example, the confrontation between Fatima Juarez, the congresswoman from the Eighteenth Congressional District in California, and Michael Schwartz, an Orthodox Jewish assemblyman from New York's Forty-Eighth Assembly District."

"Okay."

"At one of her rallies she spouted antisemitic, anti-Israel statements. Schwartz confronted her, and she had him physically ejected, to raucous cheers from her supporters."

"So? That stuff happens regularly across political lines."

She shook her head. "Look at Louis Farrakhan, the leader of the Nation of Islam. He calls Jews 'termites.' And what about Alfred Walker? He was once a Democratic candidate for the presidency, and he said Israel was an apartheid country!"

"Yes, I get it. But the world is full of examples of racism and jingoism. Many religious and cultural groups are impacted. You think Jews have a monopoly on victimization and hatred directed at them?"

Caitlyn leaned back in her seat, let out a robust quantity of air from her chest, and looked at Ash with thinly disguised frustration. She sipped her coffee.

"Here, Caitlyn, let's make things more interesting. Bernie Sanders is a Jew, right?" Her blank look gave him the answer. "He lost family members in the Holocaust, right?" Same blank look. "Is he a self-hating Jew? Does he hate Israel? How do you explain his psychology? Do you really believe—looking at this *rationally*—that advocating for Palestinian rights equates with harboring prejudice or hatred against Jewish people? Can you allow that government policies can be distinct from the ethnic or religious identities of the people they represent? Same for individual political views. I mean, for example, opposing China's treatment of the Uyghurs does not imply Sinophobia any more than opposing Russia's invasion of Ukraine implies hatred of Russian citizens. And how about groups like Jewish Voice for Peace, or Breaking the Silence, that advocate for Palestinian rights and criticize Israeli policies? Why can't it be more complicated than you suggest? And consider this: Maybe Navi Scharf is wrong and has set you down an endless path paved with unanswerable questions."

"What's your point?"

"The point is, Scharf is a mere mortal, is he not? He stressed that souls evolve over successive lifetimes, driven by the lessons they're meant to learn. I can't tell you how many times he used the words 'growth,' 'healing,' and 'transformation.' Past lives are one thing, but a complex, interactive network of human souls working in tandem to reconfigure the lives of all of us over time is quite another. Perhaps the learned Dr. Scharf is a tad Pollyannaish—or, worse, has succumbed to his own hyperbole. Isn't that worth considering?"

Ash stopped and took a seat at the kitchen table. He wore a self-assured smirk, as if he had made the chess move of a lifetime, with checkmate looming. He felt Caitlyn's stare piercing him. Her face indicated a reeling mind, pondering her own next move.

"Your argument is skewed. You're leaving out other things Scharf said... *Professor*. He did not paint a rosy picture of a universal state of souls. He appreciated and underscored the complexity you talk about. He was quick to add that bad behaviors often stem from unresolved traumas, ignorance, or karmic imbalances accumulated across lifetimes. They represent stages of learning—all souls, good or bad, will continuously receive opportunities to change. And he acknowledged that not only do souls find themselves at different points along the continuum, but they've also often evolved to different degrees. Remember what he said in the lecture: 'We humans either resolve a problem or repeat it in another lifetime.' You liked that, remember?"

"True. Although that applies *within* a lifetime, as well, so it proves nothing."

"He also said a soul that causes harm will face situations in future lives that encourage empathy and understanding. For instance, being on the receiving end of the same harm they inflicted on others. Think Ebenezer Scrooge in *A Christmas Carol*."

"Charles Dickens and Navi Scharf, peas in a soulful pod."

"Let me remind you of what happened to me during the investigation into President Uzinski's murder. Under hypnosis, Robertson got me to recognize Neil Braxton's voice in the university's Records Room—you know it's as dark as a dungeon in that basement—and it was the voice of the Auschwitz prison guard who had once attacked me. Our souls were in distinctly different stages of evolution."

"No quarrel there. But those states of being were self-evident in the present, no Ouija board needed. But you're leaving out something else he said in the lecture."

"Oh? What's that?"

"He suggested, if memory serves, that what might materialize as a 'bad' soul might be performing a soul contract. I took that to mean the soul has stepped up to do something heavy in someone else's life, to teach a lesson. Consider whether the people you label antisemites are playing that role—testing the chosen people, as it were."

"Jesus, Ash! That's such nonsense. Religious hatred and persecution has, unfortunately, never been fleeting or aberrant when it comes to the Jewish people. Have you forgotten your history lessons? Are you not paying attention to what I've been saying all this time?"

Her voice had risen, clueing Ash in that he had pushed the wrong button.

"Okay, okay, fair point."

"And let me correct you. Scharf said when that happens, it's a *temporary* thing. It does not represent any stage of the evolutionary journey or the soul's eternal essence. The truth is, evil people travel with you in your soul group. They're everywhere. Their work is splattered over American college and university campuses. So the question is, do antisemites who repeat their roles as God deniers in multiple lifetimes get to learn a lesson too? Can we reach out and change them? I need to get to the bottom of this."

A long silence ensued. Both sat alone with their thoughts, less concerned about jousting than seeking intellectual light.

Ash broke the trance. "I think you've figured out how Dr. Scharf might respond to your confusion."

Caitlyn offered up her right hand as if to say "Have at it."

"I'm betting he'd say that persistent patterns of hate, like antisemitism, reflect the collective failure of souls to learn the lessons he contends are presented life after life. They've become, as a result, deeply entrenched karmic challenges that will require numerous lifetimes to overcome... Maybe that won't happen until *humanity as a whole* makes significant spiritual progress." He released a long burst of air.

Caitlyn nodded.

Ash continued, "The point is, maybe you're out of your element, trying to put your finger on the scale."

"No, that last part I don't accept. We, all of us, have a duty and opportunity to help humanity make that spiritual progress, to push us all toward the finish line."

"So we're back to data collection through hypnosis?"

"Yes. But not yet. First, I want to create a group of connected souls. A circle of energy. A powerful force to stimulate self-discovery and enlightenment... And I need your help to make it happen."

"Where? How?"

"Good questions. But classroom duties beckon."

Ash leaned back and opened his arms wide, as if to say "You're leaving me hanging?"

"To be continued," Caitlyn said. She rose from the table, pecked him on the cheek, and darted out of the house.

12

THE COALITION FOR CAMPUS JUSTICE

Michael Unger, a graduate student in the School of Business. Mary Jean McLean, a graduate student in the Psychology Department. William Carlyle, a senior in the Biology Department. Stephen Smith Johnson, a junior in the Political Science Department. Joshua Weiss, a graduate student in the Psychology Department. Melissa Baines Rutherford, a graduate student in the Music Department. Each eagerly accepted Caitlyn's invitation to comprise a new, if controversial, coalition on campus. Ash recommended calling the group the Coalition for Campus Justice for its "optics," and Caitlyn went along. And so it became known as the CCJ.

The handpicked members had at least one thing in common: type A personalities.

Michael Unger, muscular and dark-haired, was majoring in marketing and finance. A staunch Republican, he was active in student government and an excellent speaker—he had debated in high school—and dressed the part of a wannabe leader, taking pains to consistently project a professional look. He was a Conservative Jew, and several trips to

Israel with his family had opened his eyes to the Holy Land to an unfathomable degree. After one of his visits, Unger had founded the Hillel Center at Coronado to provide social, emotional, and religious support to the small group of Jewish students on campus.

Mary Jean McLean was a recently enrolled graduate student who had transferred from Nottingham College in Great Britain. A small, thin young woman, with dark hair cropped neatly at her shoulders, she dressed like a magazine advertisement for the Gap. She held an endless supply of firm opinions on a wide range of topics, including politics, the world economy, and British soccer, and delighted in lacing her commentary with witty sarcasm. Raised Roman Catholic, McLean had zero exposure to Jewish culture growing up, and it baffled her that "such a small population could command so much worldwide drama for centuries on end." Caitlyn coaxed her into assuming the role of CCJ secretary.

William Carlyle, a student in the Biology Department, wasn't quite sure where he belonged or lined up professionally. He had been premed and completed all the required courses for medical school before deciding his calling was to perform research in biophysiology. The problem? He continued to apply to medical research graduate programs. He struck everyone as passionate about little, although no one claimed to know him well. Neither Caitlyn nor Ash had an inkling where Carlyle stood on the current crisis on campus, but Ash knew he had a curious, bright mind and had lobbied Caitlyn to select him.

Stephen Smith Johnson, in his junior year in the Political Science Department, was the group gadfly who wore his politics on his sleeves. He could often be seen reading the teachings of Che Guevera, Karl Marx, Mao Zedong, and Edward Said, and would from time to time call up a provocative quote from one of them. Tall and slender, with wavy blond hair, a wispy chin goatee, and hazel eyes, he wore baggy clothes and avoided any look that might imply convention or fashion. Stephen had his sights set on a political career, with strong leanings toward the progressive wing of the Democratic Party. Caitlyn selected Stephen for "balance" and "credibility," despite Ash's resistance.

Joshua Weiss was a prized doctoral student who, as an Orthodox Jew, regularly studied the Torah, observed the Sabbath, often attended synagogue services, and was never without his skullcap. Of all the CCJ members, Josh brought the greatest energy to the global plight of the Jewish people, combining boundless passion with the full force of his impressive intellect. And like Stephen Johnson, he drank deeply from the cup of scholars who aligned with his political views, most notably Theodor Herzl, Leon Pinsker, Chaim Weizmann, and Asher Ginsberg. His diminutive size belied the force of his personality.

Melissa Rutherford injected a different persona into the mix. Deeply passionate about classical music, she had a fiery side, which translated into sharp attention to detail, a tireless work ethic, and uncommon drive. Her intensity sometimes put off her fellow music students, and she tended to come off as aloof. But she was no prima donna. Despite her emotive nature, Melissa was more collaborative than competitive. She dressed formally when playing publicly, as expected, but otherwise dressed down—less a lifestyle choice than a way to withdraw from the magnifying glass of performance. "And deep down," Caitlyn told Ash, "Melissa is a mensch."

The Coalition for Campus Justice

A few days after being handpicked, the newly minted CCJ members gathered with Caitlyn in the large conference room in the Psychology Department. Their immediate goal was to articulate an agreed-upon mission and organize a campus-wide meeting in the gymnasium, the same venue where Bradley Markowitz had delivered what turned out to be the final talk of his relatively short life.

Caitlyn opened the meeting. "I'd like to cut to the chase. This committee is destined to play an essential role on campus in rooting out sources of injustice that fan the flames of rampant antisemitism."

She paused to see if her opening salvo had drawn any facial reactions. Only Josh and Michael nodded.

"Most students do not understand the connection between Professor Kassimali's Peace in Palestine group, PIP, and the infiltration of antisemitic activity on campus. Fewer still know anything about the Boycott, Divestment, and Sanctions movement. In large part, our mission is educational."

"May I ask a question about that?" said Mary Jean.

"Of course."

"Include me among the ignorant. What is that *movement* you just mentioned?"

"Fair enough... In a nutshell, the BDS movement seeks the withdrawal of Israel from all Arab lands occupied in 1967, including East Jerusalem; full equality for Arab-Palestinian citizens of Israel; and other protections and rights for Palestinian refugees who've had to leave what they regard as their homeland."

"Oh-kay... so what's so bad about that? I mean, why isn't that a legitimate form of protest? Is it violent?"

"Well, not violent, but—"

"Why shouldn't we, as a group committed to social justice, support this BDS movement?"

"Professor Morrys, may I take that on?" Joshua said, bobbing in his seat.

"Sure, go ahead, Josh."

"Mary Jean, you have to understand that the ultimate goal of the BDS movement is to delegitimize Israel and undermine its right to exist as an independent Jewish state. And because one of its main weapons is the economic boycott, it discriminates against Israeli individuals and companies—which, I should add, has had an adverse economic impact on struggling Palestinians. And worst of all—make no mistake—while the words they use may sound tolerable on the surface, they disguise a hostility that fosters antisemitism."

"May I weigh in here, Professor Morrys?"

"Sure, Stephen."

"Josh provided one interpretation. Another is that the BDS movement is a peaceful form of protest. Classic free speech, no different than run-of-the-mill protests in the US, where companies are boycotted because of their political activity or human-rights violations. Recall the farmworkers who, under the leadership of Cesar Chavez and Dolores Huerta, staged a boycott of the United Farm Workers, urging consumers to stop buying grapes from farmers. Or the anti-apartheid leaders who urged US corporations to divest from investments in South Africa to protest the apartheid regime. BDS is no different, and I wonder whether this committee should inject itself into a global political controversy."

"Economic sanctions have increased tensions and worsened living conditions for ordinary people, including Palestinians. Know your facts, Stephen," said Josh.

"Let's move on," Caitlyn said. "We can agree to disagree, but the fact remains that the BDS movement is a thorn in the side of Israel and the Jewish people. If we are to complete our mission, we must bring awareness to what is negatively impacting life on campus for Jewish students, whatever its source. We must become a counterpoint to balance the dialogue and raise the consciousness of our student body."

Caitlyn paused and scanned their faces, all staring at her in silence.

"And let's be honest, our administration hasn't helped. If anything, they've made things worse by disengaging from campus events and dismissing everything as free speech, as if that justifies the hatred and violent emotional abuse that persists on campus. Yes, as Stephen points out, we must support free speech. But we cannot tolerate aggression disguised as speech. I mean, do we need any better example than what happened to Mr. Markowitz?"

Joshua raised his hand.

"Yes, Josh?"

"It helps to remember that Bradley Markowitz wasn't assassinated in a vacuum, like some spontaneous expression of passion. For weeks, PIP used outside groups like Antifa to blanket the campus with flyers and paint walls with graffiti—antisemitic slurs like 'Jews own the media' or 'Jews own the banks' or 'Israel tortures Palestinian children.' PIP's rallies stirred up trouble. They pummeled the students and faculty with hate speech and threats of bodily harm, igniting fear that spread like wildfire on campus. Free speech in the temple of ideas is one thing. Action that masquerades as speech but is designed to do bad things is quite another."

Josh stared at Stephen, who stared back.

Josh continued, "And yes, when public disorder started, the general student population was silent. Partly because of disinterest, but more because there was no organized pushback or intelligent response. That's where the administration failed us. The longer the silence, the more demoralized Jewish students have become—they feel abandoned. And we have scary historical reminders of what turning a blind eye can lead to. This committee must change that."

Stephen raised his hand.

"Stephen?"

"I appreciate what Josh said about free-speech distinctions. The problem I'm having is that we're a committee for 'campus justice,' so shouldn't our mission be nonpartisan? Shouldn't we be seeking justice for all students on campus? I mean, the Jewish people don't have a monopoly on oppression. Think about the poor Palestinian people. What do you know about the quality of their lives? If education is our calling . . ." Stephen spread his arms wide and dipped his head forward as if to say "Know what I'm saying?"

"You live in a bubble, Stephen. When was the last time—any time—you saw an anti-Muslim or Palestinian flyer on campus?" Michael said.

Everyone around the table except Stephen and Caitlyn nodded. Caitlyn seemed elsewhere.

"Exactly, Stephen," Melissa said. "If we were dealing with a serial rapist, our mission wouldn't include the safety of men on campus."

"Speaking of hate speech," Stephen said, "why are we bad-mouthing Professor Kassimali? 'Cause he's Muslim? 'Cause he has a different political perspective? Don't forget, to many students, he's a hero and leader. Is this committee becoming what it wishes to eradicate?"

The Coalition for Campus Justice

Josh opened his mouth, but Caitlyn raised her hand like a traffic cop. "Let's move on," she said.

"Michael, I'd asked you to do some leg work?"

"Yes, we have fifteen hundred people signed up for the CCJ presentation in the gymnasium, and more signing up every day. One thing's for sure, there's interest."

"Great."

"Shouldn't we identify organizations to contact for campus support?" said Joshua.

"Well, I'm still unclear. What is our mission, exactly?" Mary Jean said.

"From my perspective, our mission should be to eliminate hatred on campus. And that, to me, is synonymous with advancing social justice for Jewish students, which is a *political* problem," Joshua said. "The problem has already manifested in a murder. I'm bewildered we're even debating this."

"I'm not sure I see it that way," Melissa said, shaking her head. "I see it as Professor Kassimali talking about religious freedom out of one side of his mouth and repressing it out of the other. It's about religious freedom."

"I think dabbling in religion is a slippery slope for this committee," Stephen said.

"Antisemitism is a religious *and* a political issue," Joshua said. He turned toward Stephen. "I can't believe you don't see that."

"So what you're saying is, this committee is a political and religious group that advocates for Israel politically and for Jews on campus religiously, correct?" Stephen said.

No one responded.

"From the standpoint of school rules and policies, is that even, um... *kosher*, Professor Morrys?" Stephen said.

Joshua and Melissa, as if rehearsed, simultaneously flashed Stephen angry looks.

Stephen, however, was unfazed. "So that's it?" he said, raising his voice for the first time. "This committee will focus exclusively on antisemitism, picking sides?"

"Interesting comment, Stephen," Michael said. "We know *you're* not Jewish, but a few in our group are, and it's the Jewish students who are suffering. Get it?"

Silence gripped the room. Stephen squirmed in his seat.

"Stephen, let me ask you, do you think you have the right frame of mind for this group?" William said, leaning his big upper body over the table.

"Yeah, if you're uncomfortable with Jews, maybe this is *not* the group for you," Melissa said, folding her arms across her chest.

"Wow, talk about discrimination," Stephen said. "But thank you. You've helped me understand how the Jewish students must feel."

William nodded and ran his fingers through his thick hair. "Face the facts here. This whole problem began over an antisemitic crowd murdering a Jewish speaker."

Stephen shook his head. "I think we're not understanding the potential problems, not to mention the hypocrisy, were this group to announce an avowed Jewish mission."

"Hey, I'm not Jewish," William said. "Are you saying only Jews should advocate for Jews?" He again swiped a hand through his hair. "Are you saying when Jews advocate for Jews, it's invalid? Let's put all the cards on the table, Stephen. Are you an antisemite?"

Stephen grimaced. "Jesus Christ. I'm merely pointing out the optics, that's all. And I think some of you should check your own hostility."

"Okay, let's bring the temperature down," Caitlyn said. "Let's talk about the Mount the Mount campaign."

"Mount the what?" Mary Jean said.

"The Temple Mount in Israel."

"And its relevance to us?"

"May I, Professor Morrys?" said Joshua.

"Sure."

"The Temple Mount, located in Jerusalem, holds profound historical and spiritual significance in Israeli and Jewish culture. It was built by King Solomon and later rebuilt during the Persian period. Traditionally, it was regarded as the site of the binding of Isaac in the Torah, where Abraham prepared to sacrifice his son as an act of faith. The Temple Mount is considered the holiest place in Judaism, the innermost sanctuary where God's presence dwells. It also symbolizes Jewish sovereignty."

"May I, Professor Morrys?" said Stephen.

Caitlyn sighed and reluctantly said, "Okay."

"What Josh omitted is that, while Jews revere the Temple Mount, access is highly restricted because of its parallel significance to Muslims as the home to Al-Aqsa Mosque, the third-holiest site in Islam, after Mecca and Medina. In other words, to Muslims, the Temple Mount is also a sacred space—where heaven and earth intersect, and a place for prayer, reflection, and connecting with God. Listening to Josh, you'd think it belongs to the Jews. Not true."

"How do you know all this?" Mary Jean said.

"I try to understand all sides. And again, I don't think this committee should get involved in that controversy. It seems well beyond a proper mission for the CCJ."

"I think we've strayed here," Melissa said. "Our mission should be addressing antisemitism on campus and providing a counterbalance to PIP. Stephen is forgetting that PIP is a partisan group, not a neutral or innocent one. A partisan group that's responsible, from at least a moral standpoint, for what happened to Mr. Markowitz."

"Stephen," Caitlyn interjected, "I'd asked you to do some leg work regarding the ADL, the Anti-Defamation League. Do you have that ready?"

"Of course."

"What does the ADL recommend regarding political hatred on college campuses?"

Stephen scanned the notes displayed in front of him. "Nothing earth-shattering. All obvious. Like making sure dorms have appropriate rules and an enforcement policy regarding inappropriate flyers and other postings. Working with campus organizations such as Hillel, the Young Democrats, and the Young Republicans—I'd include PIP in that category—to formulate a mutual response. Having a well-considered social media campaign, and, of course, involving the administration."

Stephen exhaled and sank deeper in his chair. The muscles in his face softened. He scanned the group, looking for reactions. The silence in the room became awkward.

Then Melissa leaned forward and lifted her hands, palms out, elbows on the table. She smiled at Stephen and said, "Thanks, Stephen. Those suggestions are doable, except, perhaps, regarding the administration. We probably should appoint someone to handle a media campaign."

"How about you, Joshua?" Mary Jean said.

Joshua raised both hands and shook his head in a "not me" manner. "I don't want the attention. I'm thinking Professor Connor. He's got a fair amount of political capital on campus. We need faculty support."

"I'm not so sure about that," Caitlyn said. She leaned back. "Let's wrap up for today with some assignments. Josh, please prepare a mission statement for our review and comment. Michael, please prepare a bare-bones outline for a media campaign."

She pushed away from the table. "Nice work, everyone. We will continue to have disagreements. That's healthy, so long as we keep civil tongues and work toward common ground. Meeting is adjourned."

As they rose and shuffled about in the room, bidding goodbyes and engaging in small talk, Stephen blew past the loosely assembled committee members without a word and swept out the door, like a strong gust of wind foretelling an ominous storm.

13

THE OTHER MEETING

It was a fifteen-minute walk from the building where the CCJ had met to Professor Kassimali's faculty (and de facto PIP) office. Stephen made it in ten. He found the office door slightly ajar and knocked softly.

"Please come in," a voice said, and once Stephen had entered, "And shut the door behind you."

The professor sat behind his desk in a gray suit with an open-collar, starched white shirt, writing in a notebook under a green desk lamp. Displayed on the wall behind him was a Palestinian flag.

"Please have a seat, Sami," he said, head down, still writing.

Stephen slid forward, took a seat, and squirmed in place to get comfortable. Professor Kassimali put his pen down, closed the notebook with a soft touch, and looked up.

"*Marhaba*, son, good to see you," he said, and flashed a warm, wide smile.

"*Marhaba*, Professor," Stephen said, tilting his head down, eyes closed.

"Was your meeting productive?"

"I believe so."

The Other Meeting

"Tell me about your fellow committee members."

Stephen provided profiles of the CCJ members—their academic backgrounds and personalities, his perception of where each lined up politically, the extent of their perceived commitment to the committee's work, whether any might be open to different points of view.

"Professor Connor?"

"He wasn't there."

"Really? What do you make of that, Sami?"

"Unsure, other than this is her thing, not his."

"I see. Still, where do you see his allegiances?"

"Hard to say. Based on his classes, I'd say he's ambivalent. He tends to overthink things and fancies himself a leading intellectual—which, in this context, might help."

"So, then, sounds like the main antagonist isn't Morrys but this Joshua person?"

"Well, I'd say the two are closely aligned. He's the classic American student pet, and I think he's got a crush on her. Politically, for obvious reasons, she's the more dangerous. As you know, she has strong standing here. But my guess is, she'll not do anything that conflicts with what he wants to do. He's deep in emotionally—smart, and motivated too. I see him as her bellwether, as they like to say in this country."

Kassimali nodded a few times, eyes down, and folded his hands into a prayer posture, touching his fingertips to his mouth. After several seconds, he dropped his hands and returned his gaze to Stephen. "The others, then? Sheep?"

"For the most part. Mary Jean McLean has the most open mind. When I pushed back on the BDS movement, she seemed to want to understand. I don't see her as an advocate for a political cause. More trying to do the right thing. She is, remember, a Catholic."

"How would you say they received you, with all of your contrariness?"

"Not well, at first. I forgot to mention... two suggested I might not be suited for the group, that I might be an antisemite."

In an instant, Kassimali's face went from attentive and open-eyed to stern and creased. He put his hands flat down on the desk and leaned forward. "Yes, Sami, you forgot to mention that. Do you understand how serious a problem that is?"

"Well, of—"

"You're of little use if they see you as a threat, and *no* use if they show you the door."

"I understand, Ammo. I—"

"I can't stress enough—we *discussed* this—it's okay to offer contrary information if delivered with a neutral tone. Like you're searching for enlightenment, not advocating. It is downright dangerous, on the other hand, to get combative or critical. Don't make it personal. Address ideas and facts. They *must* perceive you as an inquisitive young student, maybe even naïve, looking to expand your horizons. Be useful. You want to blend in." Kassimali leaned back, exhaled, and shook his head.

"I'm sorry, Ammo. It was just that Josh's misleading statements ticked me off."

"Getting ticked off is not the issue, son. You *acted* on your feelings. You let them gain power over you, and then you tried to change them. That's not happening. You're powerless. Morrys is going to do what she wants. Unlike most American women, she's not weak or whiny. She's arrogant and brash and expects the rest of us to get out of her way. Your highest and best use is to monitor and learn and not draw attention."

"I understand, Ammo."

"What're their goals?"

"Morrys calls them educational, teaching about hate and religious persecution."

"And we... we are the target? It's not generic?"

"Exactly. We're the target. They want students, Jews and non-Jews, to see us as hateful and dangerous. They want everyone to view us as morally responsible for Markowitz."

Kassimali swiveled to his left to face the window, which spanned the entire wall—an unobstructed portal into the life of the campus—and gazed at the ebb and flow of pedestrian traffic, as if seeking a revelation. After a long, almost uncomfortable pause, he swiveled back and looked at Stephen.

"*Fear...* fear is their currency, Sami. Always been that way with them. That is not our way. We fear only Allah, who is with all of those who do. Understood?"

"Yes, Ammo."

Kassimali looked intently at Stephen, who felt the stare boring into his soul.

"How do they intend to educate, as you say?"

"A major social media campaign. The details aren't worked out. Also, as you know, a major rally in the gym to stoke remembrance of Markowitz."

"Yes, I've heard of the rally. They're actively recruiting sheep."

"Uh-huh."

"We can't be idle on the media front. We have prevailed in the news-narrative war. The international media has embraced the message that we are victims of the Israeli military complex and machine. The fact that there are one billion Muslims and only fourteen million Jews has flown over the heads of most Americans and Europeans."

"They are not even unified amongst themselves."

"True. American Jews remain divided and have a tendency to undercut each other. Many, thankfully, know the difference between right and wrong, but a shocking number of Americans on the whole are uneducated and wallow in a cesspool of ignorance. They have short memories and, as any astute politician knows, are easily manipulated. Remember, this is a *political* war, and that means the ends justify the means."

Kassimali winced as if he wanted to call back that last comment. He tilted his gaze down before continuing, "Look, our main weapons are unity and truth. If Morrys wants to talk education, history is on our side. We have the truth—never forget that."

"Yes, Ammo."

Kassimali's facial muscles softened into a paternal kindness. He smiled. "You've come a long way since we first met, Sami, when you were interning in a refugee camp in Ramallah with the PLO. Do you remember my advice to you?"

"Yes, yes, of course. You said, 'Integrity is everything.'"

"And remember this too. You don't always need superior power to control outcomes. Know your history lessons: the Trojan horse strategy in Greek mythology, or little old North Vietnam defeating the most powerful military in the world, or—one that Jews will understand—David conquering Goliath. Be smart. Be cunning."

"Yes, Ammo."

Kassimali rose, and Stephen followed suit.

"*Allah yerda alek*, Sami," Kassimali said, bowing slightly, holding Stephen's gaze.

"*Allah yerda alek*, Ammo."

14

THE CHOCOLATE CHIP COMMITTEE REDUX

The next several weeks were relatively uneventful on the Coronado campus. Classes proceeded apace and student life returned to normal. As springtime settled in on the quadrangles, students could regularly be seen outside, taking sunny breaks with their books and Starbucks coffee in hand, making small talk. PIP had, for the time being, at least, shrewdly opted to drop its bombastic rhetoric in favor of visuals to infiltrate the student consciousness. Posters were all over campus—stapled to trees, taped to light poles, hung from dorm windows—typically emblazoned with slogans like:

FREE PALESTINE
DOWN WITH ISRAEL
ISRAEL APARTHEID
FREE PALESTINIAN CHILDREN

Jewish groups, for their part, had gone silent, like the rest of the student body. So had the faculty, who were more than willing, even eager, to return to academic chores, normally their lifeblood. Not surprisingly, the administration had become invisible. It seemed the drumbeat of propaganda and trash talking had numbed the entire school. The vibe could not be denied: Everyone craved normalcy.

There were, however, tremors quaking quietly below the surface. Upon receiving the UPC's recommendation, on a seven-to-six vote, to deny tenure to Professor Kassimali, President Brightson sat on the matter for an unusually long time. Then, with no heads-up, he summoned Ash to his office for a meeting, alone. There was no question, Caitlyn told him, that it had to do with Kassimali, and he should be prepared to discuss the work of the committee in great detail—advice that Ash followed.

He arrived at the meeting, folder in hand, chip on shoulder. After several minutes of inane small talk about Ash's classes and the idyllic life of a college professor, the President got down to business.

"Professor Connor, I—and others in the administration—were disappointed in some of your committee's work regarding Professor Kassimali."

Ash opened his mouth to speak, but Brightson raised his hand like a traffic cop.

"We appreciate the political undercurrents, and we respect that, at least based on the report, the committee vetted the candidacy with some diligence. We don't want to belittle the effort in any way. But the committee seems to have lost sight of Professor Kassimali's main contribution to this university—"

"Well—"

The President raised his hand again. "As I was saying, the committee gave short shrift to the financial contributions that Kassimali has been instrumental in obtaining and, more so, is likely to continue to obtain in the future. The bottom line, Professor Connor, is that, but for him, many of us, you included, might be out of a job. The man has almost singlehandedly revitalized our institution."

Ash leaned back, conveying that he understood he was to speak only when and if asked.

"Now, as you know, I have the power to reject the committee's recommendation. I don't need to seek your permission or approval. But it is quite important, given the inflamed environment on campus, that university leaders get on the same page here. You get me?"

"I'm not sure I understand what you're asking."

"I am not *asking* anything of you. I am *telling* you to return to the committee and reopen the discussion, on the basis that this candidate's application should be considered without reference to his publications in the traditional sense, but with his financial contributions as a major criterion. And I expect, given your credibility and charisma, which you know I respect and admire, that you'll convince your colleagues on the committee to do the right thing. Am I clear?"

Ash did not need a political weather vane to know which way the wind was blowing. "Anything else?"

"No, that'll be all. Thank you for making the time. I know you're quite busy."

Leaving the office, Ash thought his head would explode. In all his time at Coronado, even when he'd been in conflict with the administration on matters of free speech and tenure, he had never received such a powerful beatdown, never been so muffled. He felt emasculated and wanted to scream his protest from the campus rooftops.

He immediately shared his ignominious experience with Caitlyn.

"Wow," she said, shocked at Brightson's deft play—maybe even a little admiring. "You have to give the guy some props there." Normally, Brightson operated with tunnel vision, but this turn of events showed expansive thinking. She added, "From his standpoint, the financial angle is critical. It may be wrongheaded in terms of what's important for tenure, but he understandably fears losing the money spigot and also wants to douse the flames on campus. He does have a university to run."

Ash rolled his eyes. "So I go along and play the puppet?"

"Tough one."

"Rogers will love this."

She laughed. "Yeah, it wouldn't shock me if he orchestrated it."

"You think so?"

"Actually, no. His bark is worse than his bite. He's in love with the sound of his voice." Her advice was plain. "Convene the committee, report on the meeting, facilitate a discussion, be true to yourself, and see where it lands."

Ash was angry. He did not like being played, especially by someone he did not respect who had power over him. In truth, the more he thought about how the meeting had gone down, the angrier he became—he could easily combust and go off the rails. With loving guidance from his partner, however, Ash teased wisdom from the avalanche of his frustration. He resolved to wait a couple of days to let the dust settle on his emotions and then call the meeting.

* * *

Ash had his secretary schedule the meeting without explanation. His committee thought they were done—no other candidates were in the pipeline—and he did not want to risk boycotts or other complications. So when they convened,

The Chocolate Chip Committee Redux

Ash encountered uniform puzzled expressions, as he'd expected.

He knew he had to be upfront about his meeting with the President. "Okay, let me answer the question you each want answered—why are we here?"

Rogers said, "Duh," and chuckled.

Ash provided a blow-by-blow report of what he dubbed the "lecture" he'd received from the President. He observed several heads shaking around the table and the beaming, devilish smirk on Rogers's face. Then, without forethought, he blurted out, "Before we get into that—before we talk about Professor Kassimali's financial *contributions*—let's review the danger that Kassimali and his minions pose."

Regan Klotz raised her hand.

"Yes, Professor Klotz," Ash said.

"I've done a fair amount of looking into that very subject recently and would love to share what I've learned."

Ash noticed Rogers rolling his eyes.

"Please do."

"If we're to entertain this redo, Professor Kassimali's behavior on campus should remain a major variable, perhaps even more so than the first time we had this discussion. What he has done has directly impacted the lives of students *and* faculty at Coronado University." She set her papers down and gestured across the room.

"Okay," Ash said, raising a finger into the air. He rose and sauntered over to the coffee center, where he filled a cup and loaded up on chocolate chip cookies before returning to his seat.

"Please continue, Professor Klotz."

"This is home away from home for many students who live on campus, and they've had to endure 'Kill Jews' flyers shoved under their doors. In fact, one of the founders of the Islamic Center is Mahmoud Abdul, who lived in Israel, attended Tel Aviv University, and recommended Palestinians accept Israeli benefits and medical treatments and then let Israel die. That nasty sentiment captures the essence of this group's propaganda and what it intends. We need to get rid of Kassimali. He poses a clear and present danger."

Professor Klotz pushed her red-rimmed glasses higher on her nose and continued, "The BDS movement bathes itself in social justice and civil rights as a means of self-determination for the Palestinian people, but the reality belies the narrative. The movement is all about isolating and delegitimizing Israel and undermining its existence. They couldn't care less about peace—they're only interested in wiping Israel off the map. BDS is a tool to strengthen Palestinian bargaining positions during so-called peace talks—"

"Time out, time out, for crying out loud," Rogers said.

All eyes turned to him.

"This is not a political rally and a platform for Zionist propaganda. This is a committee meeting commissioned at the direction of the school's President to address tenure. We are totally off track. Mr. *Chairman*, you need to control this meeting."

"What do the Palestinians want, Professor Klotz?" Ash said. He peered at Rogers, who glared back.

Professor Klotz smiled. "They want a so-called right of return—after seventy-five years. They want a militarized Palestinian state. They want Jerusalem as their capital, and Israeli land and territory, especially in Judea and Samaria. A two-state solution will never satisfy them. Heed their motto: 'From the river to the sea, Palestine will be free.'"

She looked around the room and then continued, "Remember, Israel is the only democracy in the Middle East. Also remember, many Arabs and Muslims are citizens of Israel, unlike in Arab and Muslim countries, where the Jewish populations have been eliminated. Most important, always remember, Israel is the only country in the world under threat of delegitimization." Her voice grew louder. She threw back her shoulders and nearly shouted her next words. "Remember, BDS is supposed to mean 'Boycott, Divestment, and Sanctions.' It really means *Starve, Steal, and Punish!*"

"I cannot believe how far off the rails we are," Rogers said. "Professor Connor, if we don't address what President Brightson directed us to, I am leaving and inviting him to attend this meeting. This is a disgrace."

The threat froze Ash. Brightson had a clear goal, and Ash had unleashed a process that threatened to undermine him. And Rogers knew it—Ash could tell by looking at him.

"I would like to call for a vote," Rogers said, "on the tenure candidacy of Professor Kassimali, replacing scholarship as a factor with financial contribution."

"I am not done with my report," Professor Klotz said in a new, cautionary tone.

"Let's do this," Ash said. "Let Professor Klotz wrap up her report, and then we'll move to what Professor Rogers prefers we discuss."

"Not what *I* prefer. What the *President* prefers, Herr Chairperson," Rogers said.

Ash winced at the Nazi reference and turned to Klotz. "Professor Klotz?"

"Women like me have achieved great strides in Israel. Not the case in any Muslim country in the world, let alone the Middle East. That ugly BDS movement fills its narratives with antisemitic slogans that actually threaten the existence of Jewish people like me around the world—slurs that would never, ever be said about any other minority group. The hatred has infiltrated our campus and warped the lives of the students and faculty."

When she finished speaking, there was a long pause.

"Okay, are we finished with this political grandstanding? What does this irrelevant pap have to do with scholarship?" Rogers said.

Ash responded, "Rogers, we *are* talking about scholarship, Kassimali's scholarship. PIP is his scholarship. He created it. How is this any different from a product created by a professor in the School of Business, or a painting by a professor in the Art Department, or a piece of music composed by a professor in the Music Department?"

Ash surveyed the table and caught a couple of nods.

"That's ridiculous," Rogers said. "Kassimali and PIP have been on this campus for years, and the only ones complaining are a handful of Jews. How many Jews are there on this campus? We have hundreds of Muslim students. We need to cater to *all* our students, their interests and needs... but I digress. Can we talk about what brought us here today?"

Not getting an answer, he continued, "Here is what I propose. The seven committee members who voted against tenure should, one by one, indicate if they'd vote differently if the major criterion was financial contributions to the university. It's that simple."

"I reject the premise," said Susan Rothchild. "No disrespect to our President, but the UPC guidelines have express criteria. And while I appreciate Ash's report about the 'lecture' he received, I don't think the President has the power to change the rules willy-nilly to suit his political agenda. If he wants Professor Kassimali to have tenure, he can reject our recommendation as it stands."

"Hear, hear," Christian Rudman said, slamming his hand on the table.

"How about this," Rogers said. "How about we proceed to a new vote based on what the President has directed. We can treat it as a provisional vote to see what would change."

"Actually, Rogers, that's not a bad idea," Ash said. "And since we've vetted the candidate ad nauseum, we don't need to plow old ground. If the vote is the same, we're done. If not, we can debate some more."

"No. Discussion is entirely appropriate first, and called for," Rogers said. "We've been asked to reconsider our recommendation based on new criteria, and that, by any semblance of protocol, requires discussion. I'd like the floor, since I've been drowned out for most of this meeting—unless, of course, we're operating under communistic rules."

Ash nodded. "Okay, let's have a discussion."

Rogers began by reciting what everyone knew—that Kassimali had managed to bring a boatload of funds into the school. He spoke in detail about how the financing had made possible the development of curriculum, as well as some capital improvements on campus. He closed by reminding them, "Without Kassimali's achievements, many of us—you included, Professor Klotz—might be out of a job. He has revitalized the university."

That final comment seared Ash's ears and he blanched.

Christian Rudman raised his hand and Ash nodded in recognition, still reeling from Rogers's closing comment.

"I understand the criterion revision. Publications are one thing, the quality of teaching is quite another. Teaching isn't all about knowledge of subject matter. It also entails creative and thoughtful methods that inspire students to think outside the box, to question assumptions and form independent conclusions. It's not about cherry-picking facts to fit a narrative or pressuring students to embrace a preordained point of view. Our job is to empower students, not to open them up and disembowel them, imprison their minds."

With his polemic, Rudman unwittingly triggered a raging debate over the difference between antisemitism and anti-Israeli policies and teaching methods. Ash let it go, even though he realized they were diverging far off the track Brightson wanted them to take and would end up back where they'd started. He'd had enough of Brightson's political play.

And Ash had another reason for wanting to hear these exchanges. He hoped they might enlighten his personal sense of who he was and what his allegiance to Judaism should be. So he sat back and allowed the discourse to continue unabated, with all the trimmings.

Ash found it noteworthy that the longer they debated, the more balanced and less personal the discussion became. It was morphing into model academic expression in the grandest of spirits. Odd, though, how silent Rogers had become, as if he'd retreated down a deep well of introspection.

One side, led primarily by Sydney Sadowsky, argued that because of long-standing history, antisemitism could never be untangled from arguments directed against Jewish institutions and government policies. Proponents inevitably crossed the line that separated legitimate social and political commentary, on the one hand, from racial and ethnic hatred, on the other.

The other perspective, championed by Christian Rudman, was that it was irresponsible to use antisemitism as a lightning rod to suppress speech about matters of war, occupation, and human rights. Rudman, in particular, urged that when governments engaged in military campaigns that caused civilian casualties or territorial disputes, international law and public discourse should demand accountability. It was entirely appropriate—indeed, essential, he argued—to hold Israel to the same standards as other nations. And when that happened, it was not antisemitism.

At one point, Ash weighed in to suggest that well-intentioned passion could often skew objective analysis, and context and intent provided helpful barometers for distinguishing the two. Specific actions based on Israeli policies—such as settlements, military operations, or diplomatic choices—might be the target of valid criticism without invoking stereotypes. But when people claimed that Israel was evil, they were wading into dangerous waters. He could see—and here, he knew he risked alienating some members who had joined him in taking up the mantle against Kassimali's tenure—that movements like BDS were political stances and were not inherently antisemitic. But he could also see that chanted slogans like "From the river to the sea" could be seen not as a call for Palestinian self-determination but an implicit call for Israel's destruction, depending on one's base point of view.

Following Ash's comments, there was a pregnant pause, as if the assembled group had reached physical and emotional exhaustion. As the silence lengthened, Rogers raised his hand—something he'd never done—asking for permission to speak.

"Professor Rogers?" Ash said in a subdued tone.

"Look, you all know where I stand. That it's wrong to use antisemitism and fearmongering to suppress the voices of those who advocate for Palestinians. That it's wrong to isolate Jewish students as victims while ignoring students with different political views who are also subjected to discrimination. But more to the point of what this committee should be doing, it's wrong to use a pro-Israeli and anti-Palestinian political platform to deny tenure to Professor Kassimali."

He paused for breath and nodded introspectively. Then he continued, "But here's the thing. It's as wrong for the President to change the rules to give himself the political out of rubber-stamping a coerced recommendation. Yes, I still support recommending tenure for Professor Kassimali. It's the right thing to do, and those who voted otherwise are misguided. But we adhered faithfully to the established process, applied the criteria laid out in the guidelines... and voted. So, I propose we advise the President that the committee, after hearing what he had to say, decided to reaffirm the original recommendation. Our professional integrity and the integrity of this committee require no less."

Rogers leaned back in his seat, and the rest of the committee sat frozen in silence, stunned, a few with mouths open.

Ash scanned the conference room table and said, "Time for a cookie break."

Everyone jumped up, as if unleashed from captivity, and stretched their legs. Except for Rogers, who sat there, apparently in deep thought.

Ash sidled up to him, leaned over, and whispered in his ear, "Thank you for that."

The meeting adjourned shortly afterward. For Ash, the experience had transcended committee business. The discussion had propelled to the forefront his stop-and-go journey toward embracing a Jewish identity. He could sense changing winds coming his way, and his life would no longer be the same. Was he ready?

15

BURIED TRUTHS, OPEN WOUNDS

The unexpected conclusion of the UPC meeting empowered Ash as he braced to report to Brightson that the President's top-down directive had failed miserably to achieve its intended result and, in fact, hadn't budged the needle at all. "Talk about refusing to carry water," Ash would later exclaim to Caitlyn. Even worse for Brightson, Professor Rogers had emerged as a voice of reason. Funny that Rogers had effectively become a UPC swing vote. That meant, if Ash had correctly connected dots, that Brightson had lost a shill at the table.

Ash relished his role as the messenger of bad news. He resented the imperious treatment he'd received from Brightson and welcomed the chance to administer a comeuppance. It was not foreign territory. In the grand tradition of his feisty romantic partner, he had clashed with administration big shots before, and this encounter wouldn't be the last. And despite Caitlyn's earlier grudging admiration for Brightson's clever political play, as far as Ash was concerned, Brightson had crossed an ethical line and played the coward when the situation begged for inspired leadership. *No, not a problem,* he told himself. *I got this.*

And so, Ash shifted his focus from dealing with Brightson to exploring his Jewish heritage and personal journey. During the UPC meeting, he'd found himself occasionally disengaged while his colleagues discussed what constituted antisemitism. The debate had faded into the backdrop as he ruminated on all sorts of questions. Where did he personally fit within the raging cultural and religious hostilities? Should he leave teaching to undertake a pilgrimage of identity? Maybe travel to Israel, maybe transform into someone he would not recognize?

Who am I, really? What parts of me are illusion? How deep should I look? Am I honest and brave enough to see and accept the truth? Will truth cost too much, undoing things I now cherish? What will become of me?

The deeper he dove into his family history, the deeper he was immersed in the excruciating pain of his upbringing, the feelings of hate and resentment. The nightmares about what had happened between him and his father had stopped, only to be replaced with intermittent daytime flashbacks that, while less graphic and always fleeting, plunged him temporarily into dark places. He'd gone from horrific nightmares to wild mood swings. While perhaps that was an improvement, it was hardly a place he wished to occupy.

Ash loathed that cruel, merciless man with every shred of his soul and resented the continuous torment he had to endure because of him. Yet he accepted there was no escaping the memories of his violent and destructive relationship with his alcoholic father, which had culminated in that awful showdown. These were the cards life had dealt him. He would be forever haunted by the reality that but for the intervention of his sister Brianna, he'd likely have killed his father. The savage intensity with which he'd strangled his father had etched itself into his soul, a lurking beast within his psyche, poised to strike whenever rage enflamed him. Did that make him a monster? Or merely an indelibly scarred man with festering demons he needed to keep at bay? Was he a genuine threat to the safety of others? Or a shamed and vulnerable person who acted out rashly on occasion? He had, for the most part, buried these fears and gone about his business as a scholar and professor. For years, he'd been unaware of how his internal demons had quietly sabotaged his ability to commit in relationships, how they'd fed the false perception that he was nothing more than a player in the singles world. Ashford Connor had held the unofficial title of number-one bachelor on campus, fair game for students and faculty, whether married or not, reduced to a lifestyle of serial dating and relationship hopping.

That had all begun to change when he first caught a glimpse of Caitlyn Morrys at a faculty meeting, shortly after she'd started at Coronado University as an associate professor in the Psychology Department. He'd found her exquisitely exotic in her tailored St. John knit suit, a fashion statement that had set her apart from other faculty members. He'd next got an eyeful of her at the campus gym, early in the morning, around four a.m., working out on the Precor elliptical machine, and ogled her athletic build. She treated him civilly, with the common deference due another member of the faculty—an absence of special attention that did not often occur with the dashing Ashford. The lack of personal interest intensified his own. He started showing up at venues where she was likely to be found—school presentations, the gym, faculty meetings and events. He wanted constant visibility.

When she presented on tenure at a Faculty Senate meeting, referring to the administration's anti-tenure mindset as "anti-academic shenanigans," that was it. He fell head over heels for her. After the presentation, he tried to gin up conversation by complimenting her on her lecture, but she thanked him and politely excused herself. After that, he had to acknowledge that any chance of a relationship turned on the timing and play of her choice. So he backed off and virtually ignored her, thinking he'd entice her that way—a sophomoric, hard-to-get strategy that went nowhere and drove him mad with yearning.

Then he got lucky or, as he would later describe it, "fate intervened." A vacancy opened up on the UPC, which she was chairing, and Ash moved in like a moth to a flame, finagling an appointment. He flattered himself that he could dazzle the female catch of the campus with the power of his intellect and his perspective on weighty university matters, never considering that the clever and elusive Caitlyn Morrys might play him like a fiddle. She had little time for silly games, irreversibly committed as she was to her work as a college professor.

But this time, Ash had read the field well. The core work of the committee required engagement and collaboration on two subjects they both held near and dear: professorial tenure and freedom of expression. So rather than dig into his customary bag of seductive tricks—which, in any event, had gotten him nowhere—he unleashed his academic passions and let them do the talking. He couldn't have constructed a better script. The committee's work bonded them professionally as colleagues advancing the same mission and generated mutual respect and admiration. It broke the ice and gave him the green light to resume his pursuit, flashing his signature charm and impish personality. They began to see each other.

Caitlyn was intrigued by Ash, despite his mood swings and subtle neediness—which she initially chalked up to immaturity—and sometimes tempestuous outbursts about academic matters—which she dismissed as yet-untamed professorial passion. Caitlyn relished her time with Ash but kept him at a sufficient distance that their relationship remained ambivalent. Simply put, as she candidly told him, she was not sure she wanted to commit to a major relationship at this point in her career. Their intimacy deepened, however, during the investigation of President Uzinski's murder on campus, when Caitlyn narrowly avoided becoming a second homicide victim.

The progression of their relationship and growing status as an "item" on campus coincided with Ash's growing sense of uncertainty regarding his professional trajectory. He began to question his long-term commitment to an academic career. Teaching and research had long been the world to Ash. It was "publish or perish" on every university campus in the United States, and there he shined. He had research grants galore, teaching assistants, and research assistants traveling with him to archaeological sites around the world. He was the most prolific professor at the school. He reveled in conscientious academic inquiry and savored the challenge of testing propositions. He loved writing and churned out scholarly papers each year with enviable devotion. He thrived in academia.

Over the past few years, however, Ash's newfound insights about his past had suppressed the inner hunger he'd once felt for his work. His personal agenda had pushed its way to the front burner and struck him, in the larger scheme of things, as more relevant and more pressing. Work had lost its luster, and Ash felt an emptiness he struggled to fill.

He tried diversifying his physical activities, adding yoga, meditation, Pilates, massage, and even extreme gym sports. He improved his physical conditioning, but his spiritual state faltered. At Caitlyn's urging, he'd agreed to become the chair of the UPC, a position she'd held for several years, which had the added benefit of allowing her to focus more on her teaching and student advising.

Still, he brooded. He'd disappear mentally at the dinner table. His mood swings increased. For the first time, he complained about research projects and papers, rather than boasting, as he usually did. He lacked focus and sometimes winged UPC meetings, which did not go unnoticed by his colleagues. Caitlyn supported him emotionally, never taking issue with the dramatic changes. She knew how Ash's mind worked after all these years. In fact, she seemed to understand him better than he understood himself. She was nonjudgmental and loved him unconditionally, and he felt safe enough with her to show his vulnerability.

Eventually, the lack of centering bothered him enough that he summoned the nerve to sit down with Caitlyn to talk over what he should do. They convened one early morning in the kitchen over coffee. She held back nothing.

"Ash, my love, you've been running around like a dog chasing his tail. Simply put, you're depressed. You need to deal with your obvious alienation and dissatisfaction. This has gone on long enough. Stop pushing off your negative feelings. It's not working. It never works. Maybe it's time for a therapist?"

"Ridiculous. I'm not depressed."

"No? Okay. Then what are you?"

"I'm... I don't know... bored. That's it, bored. Maybe a change of scenery is in order."

Caitlyn shook her head, rose and leaned over the kitchen table, and kissed him. "Ash, you're deluding yourself. You're fumbling around, searching for something meaningful in your life. You're like one of Peter Pan's lost boys." She smiled and placed her hands on her hips.

"Really, Caitlyn? Why do you always have to turn shrink and overanalyze everything? Sometimes things are black and white." He grimaced in frustration.

"Ash, my love, you're going to continue spiraling emotionally until you face the music and accept that you're depressed. Please consider a therapist." She kissed him again. Then she turned to go, zipping up her Lululemon jacket, and headed out to the campus faculty gym.

Ash remained seated, moping. He wondered if he'd ever been depressed before. He couldn't think of any time he'd felt so adrift. But depressed? What was that like? As he went deeper inside, he thought for the first time that his love for Caitlyn, which he never doubted, was not enough to sustain him, and that saddened him.

Caitlyn had labeled him a God denier, someone with no commitment to faith. He didn't believe in organized religion. He didn't believe in a higher power. He placed his trust in science and empirical data. In what could be proven, not in assumptions made to fill gaps in knowledge, to try and explain the unknown. Faith? Pure guesswork. An emotional crutch.

On the other hand, he held the intellect of his partner in high regard, and he respected what she had to say. She was sharp as a tack and exhaustively thorough. Her insistence that he was a God denier burned in his consciousness. Could his depression, if that was his malady, be a crisis of faith? She had revitalized her life through past-life regression—it had led her to a renewed faith and commitment to Judaism. Could he be far behind? Was he being shortsighted?

His sister Brianna had revealed to him the great family secret that his father was Jewish. He struggled to accept that, especially since his mother had raised him in the Church of England. In the throes of his existential crisis, he began to doubt himself more than ever. He didn't know how or what to believe. He flashed back to Brianna telling him about his father's role in resisting the Nazis in World War II. It had shocked him so much that he'd begged off the call, but it was seared in his mind.

Then he'd submitted to Inspector Robertson's powers to learn whether he'd had a past life that intersected, and discovered that he himself might have had a role in the Nazi resistance. Could these revelations be mere coincidences? Or, as Caitlyn insisted, were they intimations of who he was, a piece of the puzzle he was assembling? The recent UPC meeting had nudged him down that road again, and if for no other reason than to satisfy his ingrained academic honesty and curiosity, he wanted to know more. He had to revisit the discussion with his sister. He went to the bedroom, closed the door, took a seat on the bed, and called his sister in Northern England.

"Ash, I'm thrilled you're *finally* interested in hearing more about Father's past history and military record. Britain deployed him with the Fighter Command dedicated to defense in the Battle of Britain. When the Germans initiated the raids on London, Father was a fighter pilot."

"Yes, yes, I know, you told me."

"But you didn't let me tell you everything. Father flew multiple missions in the summer and fall of 1940. The Luftwaffe's campaign tried to force England into a peace settlement with Nazi Germany. It targeted London's factories and terrorized British citizens with its air superiority. But they were unable to overwhelm the RAF, that's the Royal Air Force—"

"I know what the RAF is."

"As I was saying, they were unable to overwhelm the RAF with their infamous Blitz—the nighttime aerial campaign that killed thousands of Londoners and demoralized the entire country."

"Okay."

"Pilots who fought in the Blitz were referred to as the Few. You need to understand that many RAF fighter pilots, our father's comrades, didn't survive. Father was constantly surrounded by death—he had as many as fifty-seven kills, and he watched countless fellow pilots go down in flames. And not always strangers or bad guys. People he knew. People he was close to. People who were willing to give their lives for freedom. Eventually, he began drinking to blunt his fears and his overwhelming sense of survivor guilt. You getting this?"

"Go ahead."

"On one mission, the Germans shot down his plane. His gunner bailed out, but his copilot got trapped. Father stayed to try and help him, but he finally had to jump. His entire life, Father heard the frantic voice of his copilot screaming for help. He'd say he drank until he 'didn't hear Mike's screams anymore.' He not only risked his life, he risked his sanity and well-being to stop the Nazis. He was proud and loyal—that's what heroes are made of."

Brianna paused, as if waiting for a response. Ash exhaled into the receiver but said nothing.

"His family were Orthodox Jews who immigrated from Warsaw, Poland. They lived in Birmingham. Weren't you ever curious about our grandparents, Ash?"

"Brianna, I never wanted to know anything about him. I didn't want to know him. Why would I be curious about his family? I hated him."

"Can't you forgive him for beating you, Ash? Can't you forgive him even now?"

"Beating *me*? You think this is about me? No, Bree. It has little to do with me. I hate him for beating Mother! He'd come at me and she'd get in between us to protect me. I'd push her away, but she'd hold me tight and wouldn't let me go. I hate him for beating her... not me, Brianna." His last words trailed off softly and slowly, as if he was succumbing to an onslaught of emotion. Ash had never uttered those words before, not even to Caitlyn.

"Ash, I'm sorry. I'm not belittling what you went through. You were young, and what happened was unfair and painful, I know. Your hatred is understandable. I never doubted that. Not for a moment. But you'll never get past any of it if you don't come to terms with Father's demons. The war broke him. He'd seen so much death. He lost so many friends. Can't you find some sympathy for him?"

"I was angry at Mother for not leaving him. She'd stand there and take his beatings and his abuse. Why didn't she run with us?"

"Run? Where? Warsaw? The concentration camps? She had no one. Her entire family perished in the camps." Brianna began to cry.

"Concentration camps? Mother was British. She was a Christian!"

"Ash, Mother was a refugee from the Polish concentration camps. As a young girl, she was sent to a German brothel to service German soldiers—first to Ravensbrück and then to Auschwitz. She was a sex slave for years, until a German SS officer singled her out for himself and absconded with her. She survived the camps and escaped after the war to a displaced persons camp. That's where Father found her."

"What was Ravensbrück?" Ash said in a subdued tone.

"A concentration camp, basically for women. The Germans kidnapped over one-hundred-thirty thousand women and sent them to Ravensbrück, north of Berlin. Many were political prisoners from other European countries, and many were involved in slave labor at the Siemens & Halske company. Some fifty thousand perished, and the rest were shipped to Auschwitz for extermination.

"The largest national group was Polish prisoners from the Polish Underground. That included Mother—she worked in Warsaw for the Polish Underground and was captured in a raid in 1939, when she was sixteen. She experienced one horror after another—she witnessed countless medical experiments she refused to talk about. After Ravensbrück, she wound up in Auschwitz, too, before that SS guard commandeered her as his personal pet. Was she lucky, Ash? Would you use that word?"

"How did Father find her?"

"After the Allies liberated Auschwitz, he met her while she was helping nurse other inmates. She took care of him when he came down with typhoid."

"Why did she stay with him all those years?" Ash said, almost in a whisper.

"I've thought about that often. Mother loved him, Ash. She adored him. She *understood* him. Don't you get that, at least? She understood he was mentally and physically sick. After all the death and mayhem she'd experienced, it was a safe place for her. Can't you see that?"

"Yes."

"I never judged her, Ash, never. I loved and respected her enough to understand that she had made peace with herself and her life."

Brianna took a deep breath and stopped. Ash stayed silent.

"Knowing this, are you still angry with them? Can you find your way to forgiveness? They were two young people whose lives were shattered, during a horrific time in human history. Think about your Death Harvest Theory, or Model, or whatever it is that you're so famous for. 'Out of great disasters come great innovations, inventions, and steps forward in society.' Isn't that the premise of your theory?"

"Uh-huh."

"Look at the life they created together. The children they raised, the business and farm Father created. Think about all those two broken lives accomplished. And look at yourself and what you've done in your life. Do you really think you have the right to judge them? Maybe you should celebrate them. Think about that."

A prolonged silence ensued. Ash began to cry. Brianna too.

"I'm sorry, Brianna. I'm so sorry."

"Ash, you deserted us. I understand why. I get it. You had to get out from under the horror of our upbringing. But you never looked back to see how we were. You never called us. You've kept running—running away from life, from your family, from yourself. I don't judge you. You were emotionally scarred... and afraid. But it's time to stop, Ash. It's time to stop running. It's time to heal."

Ash did not know what to say. He thanked his sister, promised to stay in touch, and politely terminated the call. Then he leaned back in the bed and placed his head on the pillow, emotionally drained and physically depleted, his eyes filled with tears. He felt unmoored—he'd never before been so vulnerable and uncertain of his direction. He was facing a full-on identity crisis and profound test of character. Unbeknownst to him, the state of perplexity in which he found himself was about to get much worse.

16

THE REBECCA MYSTERY

Ash knew little about Jewish culture and Jews in general and, in truth, had never had any reason to learn. His early years sequestered him in a rural community dominated by expansive farming fields, vast skies, and scattered homes, among others who looked alike, shared a common dialect, attended the same educational institutions, observed identical religious practices, and had precious little exposure to the broader world. His out-of-the-nest breakaway schooling experience in London as a young adult had shattered these barriers, introducing him to a wide array of ethnic groups, diverse personalities, and nuanced living. The observant and bright Ash, a budding academic, quickly broadened his view of life and delighted in the richness of humanity and its different forms of expression.

But although as a young man he'd been curious—a characteristic that would feature prominently in his pedagogical career—he hadn't applied his curiosity to Jewish culture. The little exposure he had to that part of the world was limited to sightings of the distinctly outfitted Orthodox Jews who shuttled to and fro on the streets of London, attending to their own business. Coronado hadn't changed that.

Its faculty did not boast any Orthodox Jewish members, and Jewish student groups like Hillel Center kept low profiles and integrated into campus life, as youth are wont to do. When it came to Jewish culture and practices, Ash had much to learn. But whether he was poised to jump in with both feet and embrace his apparent lineage full on remained to be seen.

The challenge positioned him precariously on a precipice between two worlds: one shaped by measurable evidence, the other divined from subjective encounters. For his entire adult life, rigorous requirements of logic and testing had defined his approach to all things worth knowing. Conversely, thanks to Inspector Robertson and the irrepressible Caitlyn, he had recently encountered an unshakable vision of a past life that could not easily be dismissed through conventional scientific methods. Nor could he disregard the remarkable intersection among many recent occurrences: the eerie resonance between his past-life memories and Caitlyn's, his experiences at the past-life-regression conference he'd attended with her and Robertson, what his sister Brianna had shared about their family history, and the growing concerns about antisemitism in the day-to-day world. For all his intuitive skepticism about "beliefs," Ash at bottom was a learning sponge who never closed the door to "what ifs"—he was forever open to indulging sheer wonder. That didn't mean at the end of the day he'd step outside the walls of his scientific mindset, but that possibility increasingly loomed.

The question he faced was this: Can science and past-life regression work in tandem, each offering a different lens through which to view the world experience, or do we have to choose between them?

One evening, as he and Caitlyn sat at the kitchen table, their preferred forum for debating, Ash told Caitlyn he wanted to have his DNA tested through Ancestry.com, as she'd done.

"You know the truth, Ash. Why bother?"

"I know what Brianna *told* me... based on information passed on to her."

"Ash, this is not a scientific experiment."

"Actually, Caitlyn, it is."

"Suit yourself. To me, it's more meaningful to ponder how both of us, raised as Christians, turned out to be Jewish. And then, in a sea of billions, found each other. Scientifically speaking, maestro"—she paused to grin devilishly—"what are the odds?"

Ash smirked. "Perhaps we're guinea pigs for an intelligent-design experiment." He laughed aloud at his quip.

"Laugh all you want, but we are on to something big—and the sooner you see that, the better we, as a team, can figure things out."

Ash wiped the grin off his face and gazed at his partner, who was rising from the kitchen table to make herself another flat white coffee.

"I want to go over what Brianna told me again."

"Okay."

Ash held nothing back, sharing his innermost feelings about his parents and the beatings, those he'd received and those administered to his mother. He described his mother as "a frightened little girl" and recounted how she'd survived several years of horrifying abuse at the hands of the Nazis. The more in depth he went, the more choked up he became. When he finished, he reached across the table with both hands and Caitlyn clasped them in hers. His pout highlighted his vulnerability.

"I know what you're going to say. That I should've done this a long time ago, that I've been running from the truth... from myself." He looked into Caitlyn's stormy gray eyes, entranced by the sweep of her seductively long lashes.

"No, my love, that's not what I was going to say at all. You've been incredibly brave to venture into these past events. I know all too well what it takes to mine your family's past and shine a bright light on yourself. It pained me greatly to investigate my mother's history and search through her things. Learning about my family's history, my mother's addiction, and my parents' behavior toward their families brought me shame and sadness."

She leaned back, releasing her hands from his, and sipped her coffee.

"My mother rejected social norms—she ran from rules and mores her whole life. I was an adult-child raising my two younger siblings. Childhood bypassed me. As a young girl, I lived in constant fear of my mother's next manic episode. I walked on eggshells every day. Sound familiar?"

Caitlyn returned her hands to his, and when he grasped hers, she kissed each of his hands.

"Walking on eggshells describes my home life to a *T*," Ash said. "I never knew when my father was going to explode. There was no notice, no ramp-up. We lived on edge, trapped in a cycle of fear and paranoia. It would just happen suddenly. Like a time bomb that didn't tick out loud. The uncertainty suffocated me. I've spent my whole life hating him."

"But now at least you have context. Now you understand why. Now you can see things from other perspectives. You're informed."

"Yeah, well... a little late in the game."

"It's never too late to revisit and reassess and heal. It's simply a matter of wanting to."

Ash nodded and exhaled. "Growing up, I never knew anything about my parents' past history. I never knew anything at all about my mother being a refugee. I feel ashamed now. I've been so caught up with my hatred, I couldn't hear or see anything else."

"I admire you for wading into the turbulent water of the past the way you have. If we don't learn the truth and recalibrate, we remain blind to our potential. Our growth path gets stymied. Sure, Brianna has an interpretation of events, but it doesn't have to be yours. Her perspective is her own. But it helps to understand it and factor it into your equation."

"I don't feel very brave. I feel like a fool. I feel sad," Ash said in a hushed tone.

"Listen, my love, you deserve time to synthesize this new information. Blaming yourself for walking away from the family—a rational and healthy response at the time—will only increase your sadness and depression. Give yourself some grace. Forgive yourself first, Ash. Remember, you were a child growing up in a violent household. You witnessed the abuse of your mother. You suffered your own abuse." She paused and took a breath. "And another thing. Don't feel guilty for not saving your mother. That was not, and could never be, your responsibility. You were the child in a horrific family drama, not an adult with decision-making options. Do you understand what I'm saying to you, my love?" Caitlyn leaned forward, placed her left hand softly on the side of his head, and kissed him.

Ash lowered his gaze for several seconds. Then he pulled his shoulders back and sat up. "I'm grateful for your support. Truly. But at the end of the day, it is my cross to bear." He nodded a few times and then continued, "Your earlier comment has me reeling. About how our journeys into the halls of Judaism have been so similar—it's quite a coincidence."

Caitlyn jerked her head back, surprised. "That's no coincidence." She smiled and shook her head vigorously.

He shrugged. "Perhaps not."

"Well, for all that, at least we have a happy event coming."

"Yes, we do ... When did the doctor say you'd go into labor?"

"He thought two or three weeks. All is good."

"You know, Caitlyn, I have to admit, there's an energy here, a sense of spiritual coalescence, that's eerie. It's as if something is coming together, something greater than us."

"For sure."

"Divine intervention!" Ash said, extending his right arm outward as if introducing a new act on stage.

"Maybe our child will fulfill Jewish prophecy."

"Didn't you say that souls travel together? Is a family quest in the offing?"

Caitlyn's expression changed from enthusiastic to inquisitive. "Are you suggesting a preplanned event? That our unborn daughter is of an intelligent design, Ash?"

"In essence, that's what I'm suggesting—a predetermined event—and we'd be part of that design in some way. That would mean we'd need to figure out how to help our daughter."

"Ash, I can't believe you're saying this. You're the very last person in the world I'd expect to propose intelligent design in any aspect of life."

"Stranger things have happened."

"Explain."

"I'm struck by the fact that you and I have both discovered our families are Jewish. That they were both involved in concentration camps. That we both had past lives in the Nazi resistance. Those events cannot be coincidences, Caitlyn. That said, it's hard for me to wrap my head around this, because I'm not a religious person—as you say, I've always been a God denier. But even I have to look at these co-occurring events with a critical eye."

Caitlyn suddenly got to her feet. "Excuse me... Robertson is at the door."

"What? How do you know?"

"I summoned him. Be right back."

She left the room and came back with Robertson.

"Inspector," Ash said.

"Professor," Robertson said, tipping his head in a short bow. Without waiting for an invitation, he took a seat at the table, facing the entrance to the kitchen.

Caitlyn turned to Ash. "Please tell Inspector Robertson what you've been talking about."

"I've just discovered, after a rather torturous conversation with my sister Brianna in England, that my family is Jewish. Caitlyn, as you already know, has made a similar discovery about her own family. We are trying to figure out whether the family histories are coincidences."

"They most certainly are not," Robertson said.

Ash and Caitlyn looked at each other, wide-eyed, and returned their gazes to Robertson.

"What else?" Robertson said.

"Is it a coincidence that we're about to have a child we plan to name Rebecca?" Caitlyn asked.

"No, it is not."

"Is my relationship with Ash a coincidence?" Caitlyn asked.

"No, it is not."

"Have I been placed in this lifetime to help Caitlyn?" Ash asked.

"Ash, let me ask your question in a different way," Caitlyn said. "Did Ash choose to be in this life to help me?"

"Yes, he did," said Robertson.

"Are we here to help Rebecca with a specific mission in her life?" asked Caitlyn.

"Yes, you are," Robertson said. "What else do you want to know?"

"Will Rebecca tell us what that mission is?" asked Ash.

"Yes, she will."

"When?" Caitlyn said.

"When the time is right."

"Inspector Robertson, let's cut out the funny business," Ash said. "Who *is* Rebecca?"

"Well, that I can't tell you."

"Because?" asked Caitlyn.

"It will be up to her to tell you. It's not my place."

"You appreciate how beyond weird you're being right now, right?" Ash said.

Robertson shrugged, spread his hands in a "whatever" gesture, and pursed his lips.

"Is there anything else you can tell us?" Ash asked.

"No, not at this time. I've done all I can for the time being." Robertson rose upright, like he'd rebounded from a trampoline. "I should be going. Much to do."

At the doorway, Robertson stopped, nodded jerkily, and turned. "Professor Connor, figure out your mission. Commit to it. It will unlock everything and show you the way."

As he turned and left, Caitlyn and Ash sat staring at each other in shocked silence.

Later, when Ash headed to the bedroom, he found Caitlyn in bed waiting for him. Anxious to hear her thoughts, he showered quickly and climbed into their large, black-lacquer bed, ready to tackle what he anticipated would be a challenging exchange about their conversation with Robertson.

"Okay, Caitlyn, I'm ready for your analysis of our bizarre visit with the good inspector. What do you *think* it all means? Has the man gone off the rails?"

"Well, if you take him at face value—and I think for now we should—all the odd intersections in recent times, taken alone, might be dismissed as coincidences or fodder for amusement; taken together, they're pieces of a destiny puzzle. That's what I think we should concentrate on."

"I suppose. I'm still wrapping my head around it. Predestination is difficult to accept in any manner, shape, or form," Ash said.

"Exactly my point. It's something we're going to have to accept strictly on faith at this point, and see what future events reveal."

"Ah, that word—faith—the talisman of the perpetual searcher."

"Ash, please," Caitlyn said, her tone almost condescending.

"Give me some slack. Accepting that I've had multiple prior lives is a large pill to swallow. Need I remind you how long it took for you to sign on the dotted line? Your natural impulse was to deny, and you pushed back vigorously. If anything, I'm on an immersion fast track."

"Fair enough."

"And so you don't think I've been idle, check out what I've been doing in my spare time, putting my scholarly skills to work."

"I'm all ears."

"You've heard of the Bible, right?"

"That multigenre, zillion-copies-sold bestseller full of cloak-and-dagger, fantastical, apocalyptic sci-fi? The true literary classic full of unforgettable heroes?"

"The one and only."

"What about it?"

"Well, the book narrates a bunch of stories that I think resonate with the work of that group you're heading up, the Coalition for Campus Justice."

"Pray tell."

"It talks about how its main character—someone called God—heavily supported the Jewish people, promising them their ancestral land, leading them out of oppression in Egypt, and orchestrating a divine return to sovereignty, so they could emerge to claim their rightful status as the chosen ones."

"Meaning?"

"Meaning, my delightful partner, that God is a Zionist. The original founding father."

"'God is a Zionist.' I like it. Wait 'til Kassimali and his band of merry warriors get a load of that."

"Yeah, my thought exactly."

"Talk about poking the bear."

"Yeah, well, maybe it's time to do that."

17

IMPOSSIBLY POSSIBLE

Melissa Baines Rutherford set her book aside, took a deep breath, and ran her fingers through her unruly curls. She was sitting in the Psychology Department conference room, awaiting the arrival of her colleagues Joshua Weiss and Michael Unger. She had asked Joshua and Michael to take a deep dive into their family histories and had promised to do so herself. Now, they were about to convene to compare notes. Though eager to discuss her political research and findings, she was even more impatient to reveal the personal discoveries she'd made—and just as curious to see how accurate her hunch about what they'd turn up had been.

When Joshua and Michael arrived, the three uncharacteristically dispensed with pleasantries and took their seats, anticipation filling the room.

Joshua wasted no time. "Alright, Melissa, the floor's all yours."

"Well, cutting to the chase, here's what I now know." She leaned back, taking a moment to gather her thoughts. "As you know, I was raised evangelical Christian. When it came to religion, that was pretty much all I knew. Still, I was taught to support Israel, which always struck me as odd. I mean, why call out that country for special attention? I'd made trips to Israel with my church, but those were pilgrimages to the Holy Land, rather than demonstrations of allegiance to the people of Israel. So the idea of supporting the cause of Israel was kind of a non sequitur in my life."

Both Michael and Joshua nodded, their expressions solemn and inquisitive.

"Well, lo and behold, it turns out my great-grandmother was Jewish!"

"Whoa. Really? How about that. Did you learn anything about her?" Joshua said.

"Did I!... Great-Grandma Bell was a Polish Jew who lived in Krakow before the war. Her entire family got deported and wiped out—she was the sole survivor. She was sent to a concentration camp in Poland and later met my Great-Grandpa Tom, an American GI who served under General Patton in Germany. He brought her to Texas, where they married and she converted to Christianity."

"Interesting. What concentration camp?" Michael asked.

"Auschwitz."

"That's a total mind blow. Too bizarre," Joshua said, shaking his head.

"Yeah, it is. But what do you mean, Joshua?" Melissa said.

Joshua could barely contain his excitement as he responded, "Because *my* Great-Grandfather Mendel was a Hungarian Jew from an Orthodox family, and he, too, got deported—from Budapest to Auschwitz. He and his sister miraculously survived, but everyone else in the family perished. He later met my Great-Grandmother Angelina, a Catholic and a political prisoner from Milan. She'd evidently worked for the Resistance before and during the war but was eventually captured... and tortured." He paused, dropped his eyes for a few seconds, and continued with a lowered voice. "They married right after the war, she converted to Judaism, and after navigating Ellis Island, they settled into a life on Hester Street in Manhattan's Lower East Side." He paused again, shaking his head. "I mean, boy, what are the odds our great-grandparents would meet at Auschwitz? Think about that. Insane."

Melissa nodded. "Possible."

Michael laughed to himself.

"What, Michael?"

His smile widened.

"Spill it, Unger," Joshua said.

"The impossible is possible," Michael said.

"What?" both asked together.

"The Auschwitz connection," Michael said.

"Duh!" Melissa said.

"That's not the half of it, literally," Michael said, grinning, clearly pleased with his play on words.

Melissa and Joshua exchanged a glance before each flashed Michael an unmistakable "What do you mean?" look.

"My great-grandmother was a Holocaust survivor from Auschwitz," Michael said, his tone hushed, as if sharing a dark secret.

The other two exchanged doe-eyed looks.

Michael continued, "My great-grandmother was a Romanian Jew from Bucharest. She was deported with hundreds of thousands of other Romanians, packed onto trains headed to Auschwitz. She was sent to a work camp, and then"—his voice grew softer, weighted with sorrow—"she was sent to a brothel to service the soldiers."

"Damn," Melissa said.

"Yeah. After the war, she somehow managed to get to Israel—I've got to learn more about that—where she met my great-grandfather, a Sabra, a Jew born in Israel. My father eventually came to the US, met my mother, and converted to the Baptist denomination as an evangelical Christian . . . like Melissa. So the Unger side of my family tree is Jewish." He shook his head again. "I can't get over these coincidences."

Melissa and Joshua didn't answer.

"This is weird . . . right?" Michael said.

Joshua looked down, evidently processing. Melissa nodded to herself a few times.

Then Joshua spoke up, his voice tight with disbelief. "I'm sorry. Mathematically, this doesn't happen. Three people randomly meeting at the same school, only to find out their ancestors survived the same hell? Not even in Las Vegas."

Michael leaned forward, eyes narrowed. "You're saying this isn't random?"

Joshua straightened, his demeanor shifting. A slow, knowing smile crept across his face as he leaned in, his voice deliberate yet intense. "Exactly. Think about it. Three of our ancestors were not only in Auschwitz at the same time, which is insane on its own, but they also survived—even crazier—and their great-grandchildren have now connected on a project about antisemitism?" He spread his arms wide, his voice rising slightly. "Come on. That can't be a coincidence."

Melissa nodded. "I couldn't agree more."

Joshua glanced at the others, his gaze sharp, and lowered his voice. "My grandfather used to say that luck hadn't saved his father—it wasn't chance. He was meant to survive—a divine gift, part of something greater than all of us. And because of that, every generation that followed bore a solemn duty... to speak out, to never remain silent. Because silence was exactly what allowed the war to unfold. It was what gave permission for that godforsaken mass murder to happen in the first place."

Michael exhaled slowly and rubbed his chin, his leg bouncing restlessly. He rocked slightly in place, his eyes flickering. He dipped his head and spoke quietly, as if talking to himself. "A story that lives and grows across generations... each of us playing a role in something bigger... I don't know. I'm not sure I can get my head around that." He looked up and said, his voice tight, "It's unreal."

Melissa said softly, "*Beyond* real. Call it fate, intelligent design, divine intervention, whatever you want... but this? This *means* something. It transcends us and our families."

A long silence stretched between them.

Michael's fingers tightened around the edge of the table, pressing into the wood as if he was trying to ground himself. When he finally spoke, his voice was lower, laced with something raw. "It frightens me."

"How do you mean?" Joshua asked.

"I don't know. It's just... this is so much bigger than any of us. And if it's that big, that intentional, then... what if we don't control what happens next?"

The weight of the question settled among them. Joshua held his gaze, then let out a long breath, his expression unreadable. Michael swallowed. Melissa's gaze darted between the two men.

Then she spoke, her voice almost a whisper but carrying an undeniable force. "Guys, we need to probe deeper. We need some sort of investigation."

"Investigation?" Joshua said.

God Denied

"I think we should ask the rest of the committee to research their family histories, just as we did. I think we should find out if other members of the CCJ had relatives who spent time in Auschwitz. Imagine the impossible."

"To what end?" said Michael.

"To affirm our mission."

"Mission? Let me ask this: How do you suggest we conduct this investigation?" Michael asked, showing signs of tension.

"Privately... discreetly. We bring them in, one at a time," Melissa said. "We don't want to startle them, push them away. From this point forward, we need to be calculated in everything we do."

"And another thing," Joshua said. "We have to assume, until proven otherwise, that when we speak to Stephen, we're speaking to other people beyond our circle."

"Not to worry. I have no intention of engaging him in any substantive conversation," Michael said. "But this isn't what I anticipated when I signed up for the committee. I need time to think about what Melissa is saying and where we're headed. You mentioned being calculated? We need to be smart and... rational."

"It really frightens you?" Melissa asked.

"I don't know, Melissa. It's the stuff of science fiction. I've always kept my religion in church on Sundays. Compartmentalized... private... dignified. This stuff is outside the box, has an element of the wacko. I just don't know how I feel about it. Sorry, guys," Michael said, stroking his beard.

In that instant, a definitive double-knock on the door broke their concentration, and as heads lifted, the door was pushed ajar and Professor Caitlyn Morrys appeared in the doorjamb.

"May I?"

"Of course." Joshua smiled and rose. "Good to see you, Professor."

"As well. Hi, all."

Everyone smiled at her as she breezed into the room like she was entering an awards show, her red jacket flared back, exposing a fitted tan skirt and a tight white blouse that drew the males' eyes.

As soon as Professor Morrys had settled into her seat, another knock sounded at the door—a sharp, rhythmic *rat-a-tat-tat*. She chuckled, shook her head, and rose. The expressions of the others shifted into bemusement as they awaited the new arrival.

"Ah, he's a little early," Caitlyn said as she made her way to the door. "I took the liberty of inviting Inspector Robertson to join us. I think he could be quite helpful."

The three glanced at one another, gauging each other's reactions. Josh shrugged, Melissa smirked in amusement, and Michael's brow furrowed, deepening his already grim expression.

Caitlyn ushered in Inspector Robertson, who had dressed the part. He wore a striking dark-gray blazer with an asymmetrical cut; a pair of sunglasses hanging from the left breast pocket; a tieless, crisp, pink shirt, its collar protruding above the blazer neck; and a sleek, wide-brimmed hat à la film noir. A bottled water dangled from his left hand.

She introduced him around. Robertson smiled and nodded in response to their awkward hellos but said nothing. Caitlyn extended her hand in invitation, and he took the seat at the head of the conference table and placed the water bottle on the table. He didn't remove the hat.

"So we're all on the same page," Caitlyn began, "Melissa and I spoke recently about our ancestries. I suggested that she take a deeper look into hers, and if it turned up what I expected—and it did—that she urge Josh and Michael to do the same." She took in the three eager faces. "Um, I assume the results are in?"

"Boy, are they," Melissa said. "Want a summary?"

"Please."

Melissa looked at Michael and Joshua, who nodded robustly, granting her silent approval to proceed. She spent several minutes outlining their earlier discussion, with the other two occasionally stepping in to correct or expand on certain points. Throughout her presentation, Robertson watched her with a blank expression. She couldn't gauge him at all. Was he truly listening? Was she boring him? Had anything she said resonated with him?

"So, what did the three of you decide to do?" Caitlyn asked.

Joshua and Michael looked at Melissa, a clear invitation to respond.

"Well, we thought the similarities rang too true to be anything other than a divine calling, some greater force pushing us to act on what we're learning. Although, in fairness, Michael is not fully convinced. Right, Michael?"

"Close enough."

"In any event, we thought we'd reach out to the other CCJ members, perhaps one at a time, and urge them to investigate their family backgrounds and share what they come up with. It seemed the natural order of things."

"Inspector?" Caitlyn said.

Robertson squinted at the young adults and drank some water before speaking. "Each of you comes from different places, different families. And yet, your ancestral threads are intertwined. You are wise to see this as anything other than a coincidence. I commend you. History doesn't just shape us—it binds us."

"What are you suggesting? That our ancestors knew each other?" Melissa asked.

Robertson smiled with the patience of a parent watching a child teetering on the edge of understanding, just shy of grasping the lesson. Melissa blushed.

"Close. But more than that." Robertson leaned back and crossed his legs. "I have a strong suspicion that each of you shared past lives, perhaps in more than one time period, but almost certainly during the Second World War."

"Right," Michael blurted out, his tone skeptical, "and I was a decorated war hero."

Professor Morrys shot Michael a disapproving look, and he dropped his gaze, acknowledging the reproof without protest.

Robertson remained unflappable. "Look, it is not out of the question, Michael, that you have some heroics in your history. But this is not about that. It's about purpose. It's about picking up where you and others in your past left off. It's about defining your role in a grander mission that builds on prior generations." He took a swig of water and raised his eyebrows, waiting expectantly for one of them to speak.

Joshua took the bait. "How does this work?"

"How does *what* work?"

"How do we . . . I think you said, find our role in a grander mission?"

"First, get in touch with your past life."

"And how do we do that?"

"Hypnosis."

"Hypnosis?"

"Like your Professor Morrys did, and Professor Connor after her."

"Let me chime in here, Inspector," Caitlyn said.

He pursed his lips and nodded at her.

"I see the looks on your faces. I see the hesitation, maybe even fear—and that is understandable. Let me share my experience." She looked around, making sure she had everyone's full attention. "I used to believe that life was a straight line—one beginning, one end—and everything in between was just... what you made of it through effort and diligence and a little help and luck here and there. But now? Now I know better.

"Like you, I was skeptical about stuff like this. And, in truth, a little afraid. Not for my well-being, but of what I might learn. The idea of past lives sounded like something out of a fantasy novel, or like some psychological device to help people fill in the gaps in their knowledge, to help them make sense of the inexplicable and feel more secure about their world. But when I finally took that step—when I allowed myself to be guided into the quiet depths of my own subconscious—what I discovered was beyond anything imaginable.

"I wasn't only recalling memories, like in a dream. I *relived* my lives. I was transported. I heard my voice. I watched my decisions unfolding through people who looked like me but were in another time. It all made sense... and through it all, I was safe. Hypnosis is not losing control—it's regaining it. It opens a door that has always been there, waiting for you.

"And here's the most beautiful part: What I learned didn't just stay in that hypnotic world. It came back with me. It changed me. It made me stronger. It guided me. It set me on my next journey. The doubts I once held? Gone.

"Don't take my word for it. If there's even a whisper inside you that wonders—just wonders—who you've been before, I urge you. Take the journey. See for yourself."

Caitlyn exhaled and stole a peek at Robertson. In his eyes she caught a glint of approval.

"Thank you, Professor Morrys," Robertson said as he stood. "Here is what I suggest. I wouldn't share anything yet with your committee members. You owe it to yourselves to take the journey first. If it works for you, as I'm confident it will, it will be substantially easier to show your colleagues the way, especially with the backing of Professors Morrys and Connor." He eked out a thin smile. "Nice work. I bid you adieu . . . for now."

And just like that, he was gone, leaving behind his water bottle, three college students frozen in place, their mouths agape, and Professor Morrys, smiling to herself.

18

UPPING THE ANTE

Caitlyn left the meeting shortly after Inspector Robertson. When the door had clicked shut behind her, Melissa exhaled an extended gust and said, "Damn." Joshua chuckled.

Michael was staring into space. "So . . . where do we go from here?" he said.

"I say we let things settle a bit," Joshua said.

"Yeah, makes sense," Melissa said. "If you have time, maybe I can share some of my *other* research."

"Might as well," Michael said. "My legs seem bolted to the floor, anyway, so I'm not going anywhere. Besides, whatever you have can't be any crazier than what we just went through . . . or at least, I sure as hell hope not."

Melissa explained that the prior CCJ meeting had inspired her to do some political exploration—she'd felt a nagging obligation to be "better informed." What she'd learned fascinated her.

"First of all," she said, "the primary funding source for the Islamic Studies School building—you know, that two-story building that's a stone's throw from where we sit, interestingly enough—is an Arab NGO, a nongovernmental organization, that itself is dependent financially on the Muslim nation of Qatar."

She lifted up the book she'd brought, titled *In Defense of Israel*, by John Hagee. "This book is an eye-opener." She cracked it open and flipped to a page marked with a Post-it, ran her gaze over it, and looked up. "So far as I can tell, PIP—which, as we know, has a major campus presence and promotes itself as a cultural center to support Muslim students—is in reality a cover for the Foundation for the Advancement of Islamic Culture... which itself has political ties to radical Islamic political groups like Hezbollah. And in case you don't know this, those groups purportedly collaborated with the Nazis during World War II."

Michael looked at Joshua as if begging for comment. Joshua said nothing.

Melissa continued, "Following World War II, these groups went underground and launched a wide-reaching campaign to promote Palestinian victimhood. They referred to cities like Ramallah as 'Palestinian concentration camps' and accused Israel of creating an 'apartheid' state that oppressed Palestinians. Specifically, they argued that through its laws, policies, and military control, Israel systematically discriminated against Palestinians in all areas of life—housing, education, land ownership, employment, even freedom of movement. Critics of Israel say its treatment of Palestinians has created an 'an open-air prison.' Whatever your perspective, it's a narrative that successfully transformed much of the United Nations into an antisemitic institution. It allowed Palestinians to accumulate vast global support for their push for statehood."

Melissa took a deep breath, stretched out her arms, and said, "Here's the other thing I find interesting. From a geographic standpoint, the Arab world is not only inside Israel—it surrounds the country. It's as if Israel is landlocked by Arab nations. And based on what I've read, Arabs want to carve up Israel into smaller and smaller pieces—divide Jerusalem and create a capital for their proposed Palestinian country—which is a nonstarter for the Israelis."

Melissa carried on for a few more minutes, summarizing highlights of the book, before putting it down. "It seems to me that the BDS movement, at least, is designed to destroy Israel."

Michael grabbed the book and glanced at its table of contents. "I'm not entirely shocked by what you're saying. But I am a little surprised. I'd assumed the BDS movement was a legitimate form of economic boycott, but it seems like it might be a purposeful platform for virulent antisemitism. What do the Palestinians say in response?"

"In a nutshell, that Israel conflates criticism of Israel with antisemitism to silence legitimate dissent. BDS supporters argue that opposing Israeli policies—such as occupation and settlement expansion—is fundamentally different from opposing Jewish people or Judaism."

"And what do Israelis say in response to that?"

"It's a little complicated, but in essence, as I understand it—and Joshua can clarify—Israel views BDS not as a movement against specific policies but as an effort to delegitimize and dismantle Israel entirely. Keep in mind that BDS doesn't limit its demands to ending the occupation. It also calls for a 'right of return' that could end Israel's Jewish majority."

Melissa looked at Joshua, who said, "That's a simplification, but it captures the gist."

"Also, Michael, understand that BDS's founder is a guy named Omar Muhammed who, based on my research, has devoted his life to economically isolating and weakening Israel in the eyes of the global community. He's hoping for its total collapse—he advocated the use of suicide bombers, like the World War II kamikaze pilots."

Michael furrowed his brow and squinted inquisitively. "Melissa, did you say Omar Muhammed? How do you spell that?"

"O-M-A-R M-U-H-A-M-M-E-D. Why do you ask?"

"I dunno, sounds really familiar," Michael said, rubbing his forehead. "Where the hell did I read that name? I remember a bit ago wanting to ask you two about it, but now I'm drawing a blank."

Joshua pushed his horn-rimmed glasses up into his dark, longish hair and frowned. "I know all about those suicide bombers, Melissa. My brother was killed some time ago in a murderous suicide bombing in Jerusalem—at lunchtime, while sitting in a restaurant."

"Jesus, Josh," said Melissa. "I'm so sorry to hear that."

Michael, as if coming out of a trance, slapped the conference table. "That's it! Melissa, I remember where I saw that name... Facebook. I saw the name on Facebook!" He slapped the table again.

"So?" Joshua said. "The entire world's on Facebook."

"True," Michael said. "That's why this is meaningful. I saw the name on *Stephen's* Facebook page—he called the guy his onetime mentor. This was before our first CCJ meeting, and when I went back to check after the meeting, it had been deleted."

"Are you sure it was Stephen? From our committee?" Melissa said.

Michael nodded. "Absolutely... well, it looked like him. I, of course, had no idea who this Muhammed guy was and thought nothing of it at the time. And the deletion is suspicious."

"Oh my God, he's a terrorist!" Melissa said. "I never trusted Stephen. I called him out, remember? He's an antisemite, he advocates the destruction of Israel. I knew it!"

She was shouting so loudly that both Michael and Joshua recoiled in their seats.

"Well, what should we do about him?" Michael asked.

"I say we don't do anything," Joshua said.

"Why not, Josh?"

"Because, Michael, first, we aren't entirely sure what's going on with him. And second, if he's a bad apple, some kind of plant, we don't want him knowing what we know until the time is ripe. We can keep him at a safe distance for now and try to figure out who sent him, and with what specific agenda."

"C'mon, Josh, it's Kassimali," Melissa said. "How can it be anyone else?"

"Maybe, maybe not. The worst thing we can do is be wrong and shoot ourselves in the foot, jeopardize everything. Keep messaging in mind. It was you, Melissa, who showed us how Palestinians used clever messaging to obtain the high ground around the world, despite all the evidence to the contrary. Look, perhaps as a Jew I'm paranoid. But we'd be well-advised, I think, to proceed with caution."

"Jews are not paranoid, Josh. People want to marginalize and kill them."

"Trust me, of that I'm sure," Josh said, looking at Melissa as if to say "Really?" "But we need to keep our cards close to the vest and play them for the greatest return. Which, for now, means biding our time."

"Fair point. We have enough to indicate a possible problem. What're we going to do about that possibility?" Michael asked.

"We need a well-thought-out plan to investigate Stephen. We can worry about PIP later, when we have some control over what's happening with CCJ," Joshua said.

"Okay, so we at least agree not to confront Stephen?" Melissa asked.

Joshua nodded and Michael thrust both his thumbs in the air.

"Do we share this with the other committee members?" Michael asked.

"Absolutely not!" Melissa said.

"Why not? The more people involved, the easier our research will be," Michael asked.

"Because the more people who are involved, the greater the risk of someone slipping up, intentionally or unwittingly, and letting Stephen in on what we're doing. We need to manage the process for now, just like Inspector Robertson suggested," Joshua said.

"I feel like I'm undergoing CIA training... Should we at least tell Professor Morrys about all of this?" Michael asked.

"Yes, I think we should meet with her privately. She'll know without being asked to keep this under wraps for now," Melissa said.

"And what about us? Have we become a self-appointed subcommittee? Are we going too far outside our permitted zone?" Joshua asked. "Now that we're keeping secrets from our colleagues, I worry that this might blow up in our faces."

"First, let's do some more digging into this Muhammed character and his connection to PIP and Kassimali. And, of course, Stephen. Michael, you're our social media guru. Can you handle it?" asked Melissa.

"Sure."

Melissa stood and began collecting her things and reloading her shoulder bag. A knock on the door stopped her movements and yanked the three heads up. They all watched, dumbfounded, as Stephen poked his head inside. Professor Connor was standing behind him, peering anxiously over Stephen's shoulder.

"Hi, may we come in?" Stephen asked, and entered before anyone responded. Ash followed close behind and raised a hand in the air to greet everyone. Each reciprocated.

"I was hoping to find Professor Morrys," Ash said.

"She stopped by briefly and left."

"Well, then, pardon the interruption. See you good souls around campus."

And with that, Ash left in a flash. A chilly, awkward silence followed.

Stephen broke the ice. "I didn't realize we had a committee meeting scheduled for now," he said, his tone laced with sarcasm. "Professor Connor mentioned he was looking for Professor Morrys, so I figured I'd tag along for the walk and say hello." He grinned, a sardonic glint in his eyes. "Is this some kind of secret meeting? Like the star chamber?"

"We were just going over some things."

Stephen glanced at each of them in turn, a frown creasing his brow, before his lips curled into a smirk—like he was a parent catching kids with their hands in the cookie jar.

"So, you're all here—together—without the rest of the committee? And you didn't think to invite the rest of us?"

Michael shifted in his chair. "It's not like that, Stephen. We were just, you know, discussing logistics... that's all."

Stephen's voice sharpened. "Logistics?" The word hung in the air like a challenge. "This looks less like logistics and more like a little... covert activity. Care to explain? You guys working for the CIA? Or, perhaps more appropriate, Mossad?"

Melissa cleared her throat. "Stephen, you're overreacting. We just had an informal meeting to discuss how to gather more information for the committee. We ran into each other on campus, and none of us had anything pressing to do, so we thought we'd make good use of the time on our hands."

"Informal?" Stephen's eyes narrowed. "About what? You couldn't trust me with your *informal* thoughts?" He stepped closer to the table, his body tense. "Come on, now, fess up. What's going on here, huh? Who decided I wasn't trustworthy or dignified or Jewish enough to be part of this little cabal?"

"Stephen, take a seat. Join us," Joshua said. "We were thinking about surveying trends at other colleges regarding tensions on their campuses. In the aftermath of Markowitz's murder, it's a topic of interest to the CCJ. Your timing is gold... Maybe you can handle part of the assignment."

Stephen looked at them in disbelief.

Michael weighed in. "Let me ask you something, Stephen. What do you know about your great-grandparents?"

"What?"

"For example, what did they do?... Where were they during World War II?"

At the question, Stephen's countenance softened. "Why do you ask?"

"I find family background fascinating."

"Okay." Stephen cast them all a suspicious look. For the first time since he'd showed up, he seemed unsteady on his feet. "My great-grandmother was sent to Auschwitz in 1941. She was hidden by the nuns at St. Mary's Catholic Convent in Berlin for years, until the SS raided the place. Someone had apparently leaked that children were hiding in the tunnels under the old church. And my great-grandfather was a Russian soldier who was held in Auschwitz and liberated by the Red Army in 1945. He'd fought on the Eastern Front, and the Nazis said he was a Jew and beat and tortured him until he confessed. How's that? Satisfied now?" He shook his head.

No one said a word.

"I'll see you all at the next meeting... if I'm invited, of course." He marched out the door and slammed it shut behind him.

"Shit," said Melissa. "That didn't go well."

"Not so sure," said Joshua. "It was awkward as hell, no doubt. But we can't toss aside the significance of his family history. That was huge. For a moment there, I felt connected to him—and he to us, I think. His feelings were hurt. Big deal. He'll get over it."

"Either that," Michael said, "or he'll avenge the slight."

19

THE SOUL CIRCLE

A sh had arrived at a pivotal turning point. His past-life-regression session with Inspector Robertson, coupled with his sister's disclosures about their father, had triggered a profound emotional transformation—a seismic shift in how he viewed himself, his history, and his family. It was no longer just about forgiving his father for the rampant abuse. It was also about recognizing a deeper connection with him—a previously unimaginable prospect. In a past life, Ash had been a brave young member of a resistance group fighting the Nazis. His father had, during that same time, been a fighter pilot battling the Nazis—a resister in his own right, a war hero.

His father had faced evil, fought it and survived, and dealt with his emotional wounds the only way he knew how. By accepting that reality, Ash found not just understanding and empathy, but purpose—a call to continue his father's fight, and an intensely personal bond with his father that had never before seemed possible. He realized now that past-life regression was more than a window into the self, a deep gaze into the soul. It could be a tool for shaping a better world. It had empowered him to lead the charge for transformative future action. Now, he had to convince the CCJ members to embrace the path he and Caitlyn had embarked upon and submit to past-life regression, so they all could discover how their souls were interwoven together.

He gathered the full committee membership at midmorning on a Saturday, in a rarely used conference room at the far end of campus. Caitlyn joined them, bringing a hoard of chocolate chip cookies and pastries for the occasion.

Ash's first hurdle was opening everyone's eyes to the power of past-life regression. It was more than a provocative topic for cocktail parties. It was integral to human existence—and in the current circumstances, an imperative. He launched into the speech of his life.

"I've always prided myself on being man of reason. A man of logic, of facts. To me, the world was a machine—cogs and wheels turning in predictable patterns, no room for the mystical, the unexplained. Past lives? Souls? That was the stuff of fairy tales, of wishful thinkers who grasped at meaning where there was none, simply to feel secure in their unstable world." He paused to gauge the attention around the table and found all eyes eagerly watching him. "But now... now I know better."

He shared his personal transformation—how it had been unlike anything he'd experienced and how it had filled him with refreshing optimism, a new dawn. "I admit, at first I viewed the past-lives thing as some childhood fascination—as if I were a child in a make-believe world, waiting for a cartoon character to blink and break the spell. I kept thinking it couldn't be real—I understand if you feel the same way. But I kept telling myself... if it was real—if what I saw in my session with Inspector Robertson was more than just a hallucination—then what else was I wrong about?" He smiled ruefully. "It was a terrifying thought."

He took a long pull from his water bottle, and when he had finished, he saw that every eye around the table, including Caitlyn's, remained fixed on him.

He continued, "What did it all mean, I kept asking." He paused for dramatic effect and leaned back. "It means death isn't the end, my friends. It means life isn't a straight line, a single spark flickering out into nothing. It means I've been here before, and I'll be here again. It means all the pain, all the mistakes, all the love—none of it is wasted. None of it is lost. It means if *I* have been here before, so has everyone else—and that not only fascinates me, it consumes me." He slowly scanned the table, ensuring he made eye contact with each person, slowly and definitively.

The room vibrated with anticipation.

"Ponder the prospects. How many others have walked through life haunted by ghosts they couldn't see, carried wounds from battles they didn't remember? How many people have suffered without ever knowing why—without ever knowing that their pain wasn't theirs alone, but the echoes of something older, deeper?

"Folks, wars have been fought for centuries, for millennia. For those of you who have studied history, you well know how much blood has been spilled in the name of borders, beliefs, vengeance—hatred passed down like an unavoidable inheritance.

"But what if... if it's not hatred? What if it's memory? What if the anger among nations, religions, and people isn't just ideology or the struggle for power, but something deeper? *Older?*

"Consider this—what if the Israelis and Palestinians of today are still locked in a war waged between them lifetimes ago? The same souls returning to the same battlefield again and again and again, a maddening cycle of pain and torment? What if the deep-seated resentments of race, of caste, of country, were not born in this life, but are being *relived* from another? What if we're trapped in a cycle of death and rebirth, because no one has ever stopped to *look*?"

Ash's demeanor suddenly shifted. When he spoke again, his voice was lower in pitch, serious and measured. "What if past-life regression could stop it? What if people could *see*? What if they could see that the enemy they hate was once their brother, their child, their lover? What if they could see that their pain, their anger, their war, is all an echo? What if leaders, instead of sharpening their knives and rallying their armies, could be shown the truth? Could be *forced* to remember?"

Exhausted, Ash paused to catch his breath. He met Caitlyn's gaze and in her eyes saw love and admiration. In that moment, he knew what she'd seen and he'd felt—that he'd commanded the room without yielding to doubt; that he hadn't been speaking to impress, as he'd done so often in his lectures, but to persuade, with conviction and genuine passion; that he'd held the committee members spellbound, not because of his stature as a popular professor, but because of the unrelenting power of his words. Caitlyn's pride radiated, flushing her cheeks. A small smile ghosted the edges of his lips before he pressed on.

"I spent my whole life believing in hard facts. In things that could be measured, proven. But the proof hit me not in numbers or formulas, but in *knowing*."

He leaned back and breathed deeply in and out, his chest rising and falling conspicuously, and then took a long swig of water. He looked around the table and saw hungry faces begging for more.

"I can no longer stand by in silence and do nothing. I see it now: a world where past-life regression isn't a curiosity, a parlor trick for the spiritually inclined, but a tool—no, a *weapon*—for peace.

"If world leaders could see. If soldiers could remember. If the wounded could heal. If everyone, everywhere, understood that the war they wage today might have been the war that took their son, their mother, their love in a time long past. If humanity could wake up from its own forgotten history, maybe the cycles could finally be broken and new ones could take their place."

He concluded, "I will never be the same again—and if *we* act together, if *we* go forth with courage and commitment, neither will the world."

In the silence that followed, those final words, a call to action, continued to swirl in the air around the room. No one moved. No one spoke. It was as if the weight of what they'd heard had momentarily robbed them of the ability to do anything but sit in stunned reflection.

Ash stood, his presence still commanding. He stared at the pile of chocolate chip cookies on the credenza several feet away. Then he smiled to himself, declining to indulge.

He returned his attention to the assembled group. "Professor Morrys will take it from here. I hope to see you all tomorrow at Inspector Robertson's home." He strode out without another word.

* * *

The next day, as previously arranged, the committee members and the two professors drove in three cars, caravan style, to the home of Inspector Robertson. When they'd settled into the fold-out chairs Caitlyn had secured from the school under some false pretense about a field trip, Ash noted someone missing. He sidled up to Caitlyn.

"Sweetie, where's Stephen?" he whispered.

"I thought he was coming, but Melissa said he decided not to participate."

"Interesting."

After they'd exchanged pleasantries and Ash had given some background, he turned the floor over to Robertson.

"First, I want to commend you all for coming. You are each brave souls." Robertson cast them an approving, paternal look. "Skepticism about past lives is natural, as is innate curiosity, especially when you feel a connection to something beyond what you can explain. It's understandable to feel apprehensive."

He paused, and Ash and Caitlyn smiled at each other, implicitly acknowledging a tone of voice they'd never heard from Robertson before, a warmth that contrasted with his normal sardonic edge.

"But I assure you, hypnosis is not mind control. You will not be unconscious. You will not lose yourselves."

Melissa leaned forward and raised her hand. Robertson nodded at her.

"But what if we see something... horrible? Something we can't unsee?"

"That's a valid concern, Melissa," Robertson said. "The subconscious mind normally has a way of revealing only what you're ready to face. But if a memory becomes too intense, I will guide you out of it gently. You will always have the ability to come back to the present moment, safe and aware. I will always be there for you."

Joshua raised his hand.

"Yes, son?"

"I've read that past-life memories can be traumatic. What if we remember dying?"

Robertson responded in the softest of tones. "Death in past-life regression is rarely traumatic in the way you might think. When it happens, most people describe a moment of peace, even detachment, as if they're watching from a distance. There's no physical pain—only understanding. And to repeat, you're never alone in this. I will be with you every step of the way. I can't overstate the safety of the process. It's important that you accept that."

"How do we know we're not just making it all up?" Michael said. "Our brains filling in the blanks with things we've read or seen in movies?"

"Fair question, Michael. This might be a little harder to grasp." Effortlessly, Robertson transitioned into an academic tone. "The conscious mind does try to interpret what it doesn't understand. But what surprises most people is the level of detail—historical accuracy, emotions they never imagined experiencing. Sometimes, people speak in languages they've never studied. The mind is vast, Michael. Sometimes, what it remembers is far more than what it has learned in this life.

"I would add this, though. Memories that arise can be symbolic, metaphorical, or influenced by your subconscious mind. It is unclear whether these memories are truly past lives, imagination, or a blend of both. We will know more when we compare notes afterward. In other words, the proof is in the pudding, as they say. When the results are in, the question will be whether what you've each learned and shared is a collection of unexplainable coincidences or something far more meaningful, something shrouded in fate."

"What if we find out something we don't like?" said William. "Like... what if we were someone terrible?"

"We are all many things across many lives, William. A soldier, a poet, a healer, a leader, perhaps even someone who made bad mistakes. But you are not just one life—you are the sum of all you have been. And with understanding comes healing. This is not about judgment. It is about discovery, about learning why certain patterns, fears, or connections may persist into your present life.

"I want to add one more thing. Earlier, I called each of you brave souls, and that you are. But you're so much more than that. You are luminous threads in the vast tapestry of existence, essential souls chosen for a sacred purpose." He stopped, a smile playing at the edges of his mouth, as if congratulating himself on a crafty turn of phrase.

"The journey you are about to embark upon is not just an exploration of memory—it is a catalyst for change. What's happening here, in this moment, is not just personal—it is a vital step in the evolution of humanity itself."

The room went silent. A candle flickered, casting shadows against the bookshelves.

Finally, Inspector Robertson clasped his hands together. "Okay. You will go in one at a time. I know you each brought reading material to occupy yourself while you're waiting. And I believe Professor Connor told you earlier, but if not, I will—after your session, please don't share what you've learned. I will facilitate that once we are reunited as a group. Remember, too, that the experience is yours alone, and what you choose to share afterward is entirely up to you. If you don't want me to share something you learned, you can tell me. My job is to guide you, to help you access the deeper parts of your mind, and to ensure that you remain safe and in control at all times."

They all released a collective breath. The anxiety hadn't disappeared, but it had softened.

Inspector Robertson stood and gestured toward the adjoining study, its door slightly ajar. "Shall we begin? Who'd like to start?"

Joshua swallowed hard, stood, and nodded. "That would be me."

The historical excavation had begun.

* * *

As they had planned, Ash and Caitlyn left the home to explore Robertsons' sprawling estate, which it turned out boasted a few hiking trails. They walked mostly in silence, enjoying each other and their surroundings. Both were drained, emotionally and spiritually. At some point, though, they made small talk and reviewed the details of the impending arrival of their child—they were planning a water birth.

It seemed like they'd been out less than an hour when Ash's phone pinged. "It's Robertson. They're ready for us."

"Wow, so soon."

They looked at each other with trepidation.

"God almighty," Ash said, "I hope this didn't blow up in our faces."

"Keep the faith, my love, keep the faith."

* * *

The five students sat in a loose semicircle in the middle of the room, their bodies bespeaking exhaustion. Each seemed caught in a strange, suspended stillness, as if the emotional toll of the past lives they'd just uncovered had left them unable to move. Melissa was hunched forward, hands clasped tightly in her lap, head down. Joshua looked fragile and haunted, his eyes fixed on the ceiling, as if searching. Michael sat with arms crossed, his posture rigid, his jaw clenched. William sat near the window, his gaze unfocused. Mary Jean sat on the edge of her chair, legs crossed, eyes wide with a deep sadness.

The atmosphere felt as if it was holding its breath, waiting for the inevitable release of tension. But they were all too lost in their own memories, in their own emotional turmoil, to speak. The silence was thick with unsaid words, with the weight of what they'd uncovered—about themselves, the world, and the collective trauma they now knew they shared.

The front door opened softly and the faint sound of footsteps approached. Seconds later, Ash and Caitlyn appeared and found seats without a word.

Once he had everyone's attention, Robertson began, this time using a notepad full of copious notes. "I am honored to be in front of such courageous souls. I truly am. What just occurred is beyond anything I've experienced in this realm. And none of this could have happened were each of you not who you are."

He let that settle before resuming, "As each student underwent their regression, vivid memories emerged, revealing a shared history of resistance during World War II. Your past identities, scattered across different regions and roles, painted haunting yet inspiring pictures of your fight against the Nazi regime. Some lived to tell the tale, others perished for the cause—but all played an integral part in the resistance.

"Here is a summary: Melissa was Élise Fournier, a French resistance courier who was captured and executed. She moved through the shadows of Nazi-occupied Paris, smuggling weapons and intelligence between resistance cells, using coded messages hidden in books and pastries. She had a constant fear of discovery and suffered breathless nights hiding in safe houses. One of her final memories is of a rainy night near Montmartre, when Gestapo agents swarmed the café where she was supposed to meet a contact. She remembered the cold steel of handcuffs, the suffocating walls of a prison cell, and the sharp pain of interrogation. Elise was executed at Fresnes Prison, just months before the liberation of Paris.

"Joshua's regression transported him into the body of Arthur Calloway, a British intelligence officer embedded deep within Nazi-controlled Germany. He'd been recruited into the Special Operations Executive and tasked with sabotaging supply lines, gathering intelligence, and coordinating with German dissidents. His work was dangerous—he remembers the paranoia of being a double agent, the sting of close calls, and the coded radio transmissions sent in the dead of night. One of his most striking memories is of infiltrating a high-ranking Nazi official's residence, posing as a translator while gathering intelligence on troop movements. The tension, the weight of a concealed pistol, the moment his cover was almost blown—Joshua felt it all as if it had just happened. He was extracted with the help of the Russians via an underground network of defectors, but the guilt he felt over those he couldn't save followed him the rest of his life.

"Michael's past life revealed the internal resistance within Germany itself. As Hans Richter, he was an engineer forced to work in a munitions factory. But instead of blindly obeying, he actively sabotaged production—weakening weapons, delaying shipments, and smuggling information to resistance cells. One of his most powerful memories is of standing in the factory and deliberately misaligning machinery, knowing that if he was discovered, it could cost him his life. The quiet acts of defiance escalated—stealing documents, planting explosives, even assassinating a Nazi officer. But betrayal came from within. A fellow worker, threatened by the SS, turned on him, and the Nazis transported him to Dachau, where he endured brutal torture and was publicly executed. His last thoughts were of the unfinished work and the hope that others would continue the fight.

"William's session plunged him into the life of Tomasz Kowalski, a leader in the Armia Krajowa—Home Army—Poland's underground resistance against the Nazi occupation. He coordinated attacks, smuggled Jews out of the Warsaw Ghetto, and led guerrilla-style assaults on German outposts. His most vivid memory is from the Warsaw Uprising of 1944, when Polish fighters attempted to reclaim the city. Tomasz led a squad through the bombed-out ruins, engaging in street battles, ambushing Nazi patrols, and witnessing the brutality of the SS. He remembers fire consuming buildings, the screams of the wounded, and constant hunger and exhaustion. In the final days of the uprising, Tomasz was gravely injured in a firefight. Too weak to escape, he was captured by the SS and executed alongside his fellow fighters. His sacrifice, however, remained a beacon of defiance against tyranny.

"Mary Jean's session revealed that in a past life she was Evelyn Whitmore, a bold and relentless journalist who initially traveled to France to report on the Nazi occupation but became deeply involved in the resistance. She started out covering the war but soon turned into an active participant—smuggling Jewish families across the Pyrenees, coordinating with underground networks, and using her press credentials to gather intelligence. She remembers a night at the French-Spanish border, guiding a family through the treacherous mountain paths. The sheer terror evoked by the Nazi patrols sweeping the area, the desperate whispers of refugees praying for safe passage—it all flooded back as if she was reliving it. Evelyn escaped in 1943, after the Gestapo began hunting her. A last-minute warning from a contact allowed her to flee into neutral Switzerland, where she spent the rest of the war advocating for refugees and documenting Nazi war crimes. She survived—but never forgot those left behind.

"Through these sessions, all of you—Melissa, Joshua, Michael, William, and Mary Jean—realized that your past lives were not just about resisting the Nazis, but about standing against oppression in all forms. Your courageous sacrifices and the moral dilemmas you faced in those lifetimes mirror the conflicts you face now in your modern struggle for justice. Whether or not your past selves survived, you all carried the same mission across time."

Robertson stood and exhaled and scanned the room.

"You all together create a spiritual force of energy—a Soul Circle. You will need Stephen to complete the circle—but we will deal with that later."

Melissa sat up straight and shouted, "Stephen? Stephen is a traitor to our cause. He's working for Kassimali's antisemitic organization... BDS!"

"I hear you, Melissa. We can take a look at that later as needed. Like all the other university campuses—Columbia, NYU, Berkeley—we will follow the money. However, for now, armed with your new spiritual awareness, the question remains: What will you do now with your new knowledge?"

20

SHOES DROPPING

It was six a.m., the sky a deep, inky blue, dawn barely brushing the horizon. The campus was eerily quiet—only the distant hum of streetlights and the occasional rustling of leaves in the chilly wind disturbed the silence.

Inspector Robertson strode across the damp pavement. He was dressed for the chill—a dark trench coat, a wool cap, and sturdy boots. His hands were jammed deep in his coat pockets and his shoulders drooped in a weary posture indicative of long nights without sleep, but he moved as if he were running a foot race. Beside him, another dark figure, smaller in stature, was keeping pace in the shadows—hands also jammed in pockets and shoulders hunched, his coat collar up and his wool cap pulled low over his forehead, obscuring his face.

"You know what this looks like?"

Robertson kept his eyes straight ahead and said flatly, "Like we're trying to avoid a crowd?"

The other person shook his head. "A tad unorthodox, dontcha think?"

Robertson stopped suddenly and turned to face his companion. "You're under orders, above my pay scale. Do what you wanna do. But once the sun's up, this campus is gonna wake up to breaking news, and the world's gonna pick sides fast."

The other man's face was stony and he gave no response. Robertson shook his head.

They resumed their hasty pace toward the administration building looming ahead. Once they'd entered, they made their way to the office of President Clifton Brightson.

The office was dimly lit, the glow from a desk lamp casting long shadows. Bookshelves lined the walls, filled with academic tomes and framed photographs of past university events. At the large mahogany desk sat President Brightson, his gray hair combed neatly back, his face tense, his fingers steepled as he readied himself for what was coming.

When Brightson caught sight of Robertson's adjunct, he jerked his head back and glared at Robertson. "Stephen Johnson! What's he doing here? What in God's name is going on?"

"He's along for the ride. I must leave it at that."

Brightson gazed at Johnson and shook his head, but Johnson didn't flinch.

Brightson returned his gaze to Robertson. "Very well. Please... um, both of you... have a seat."

They settled into the guest chairs across from Brightson. Robertson cleared his throat and leaned back. Johnson crossed his legs and looked at Brightson with a self-satisfied air.

Brightson addressed Robertson directly. "What's going on that we need to meet under cover of darkness—*urgently*, as you put it?"

"The police have arrested a murder suspect."

"Well, that's certainly wonderful and welcome news. But a phone call would have sufficed. No need for this ceremonial display at this godforsaken hour."

"It's one of your students," Robertson said matter-of-factly.

Brightson's eyebrows shot up, his jaw slackening for a brief moment. Then his body went still and his face settled into a stoic mask. "You're telling me a student—one of *our* students—murdered Mr. Markowitz?"

"Yes... Omar Ghazi, a junior. He's in custody."

"*Ghazi?* That can't be. He's one of our most talented students. I mean... he's in line to become valedictorian next year."

Brightson looked away toward the large window to his left, a gateway that allowed him to quietly observe the ebb and flow of campus life beyond. Robertson glanced at Johnson. An uncomfortable silence intruded. No one moved a muscle.

Brightson returned his gaze to Robertson, then rose and went to the window, folded his hands behind his back, and peered out at the inaudible campus, still cloaked in darkness. He spoke without turning around. "What's your proof?"

"Well, for starters, CCTV footage placed him at the scene, running away at a panicky pace, right after Markowitz was stabbed, a shiny object draped at his side. We have an eyewitness who heard a heated argument between them earlier that day, when Ghazi threatened 'to end your evil campaign against the Palestinian people... once and for all.'"

Johnson chimed in, "It's more than that, President Brightson. This wasn't some random act of violence. Not only was Markowitz targeted, but Ghazi is also much more than a misguided student caught up in campus politics. He has a sordid history."

"What sort of *history*?" Brightson said, turning around to look at both men.

"Ghazi spent three summers abroad, including in a camp tied to a known militant group. We have intelligence linking him to organizations that openly call for violence against Israel and its supporters. He's attended private meetings off campus with individuals who are under federal surveillance." Johnson leaned back.

Still standing, still looking out the window, Brightson responded, "That's hardly the stuff of homicide. It's purely circumstantial. Plenty of students travel for political or humanitarian reasons. That doesn't make them murderers."

Johnson smirked. "Sure. But most students don't have encrypted messages on their devices celebrating attacks on civilians. Or friends with ties to designated terrorist groups."

Brightson stiffened, his jaw tightening. He returned to his seat. "Do you have proof of that?" he said, looking at Robertson.

"We're working on it," Robertson said. "What we do have is enough to show that Ghazi wasn't just some angry student caught in the moment. He's been radicalized. And we have text messages from Ghazi, statements like 'Markowitz disappearing soon' and 'Elimination with prejudice to restore balance.'"

"Anything else, Inspector?" Brightson said in a tone that made it clear he wanted the meeting over.

"Yes, actually. We're still sorting out whether he acted alone, but we have reason to believe some members of PIP were involved."

"That's a serious accusation. You're talking about students—kids."

"Kids don't stab a man three times in the chest and leave him bleeding out on the ground," Johnson said.

Brightson exhaled sharply, keeping his gaze on Robertson, as if Johnson weren't there.

"Police found a manifesto among Ghazi's things. It doesn't read like student activism. It reads like a justification." Johnson's voice betrayed frustration.

"PIP is radical, sure, but this... this is something else. They push boundaries. They challenge ideas. It's healthy dialogue," Brightson said, his gaze still fixed on Robertson.

"They didn't challenge Markowitz's ideas, President Brightson. They silenced them," Johnson said. "And in an environment where it was hardly surprising that the next provocation could lead to violence."

Brightson jerked his head hard toward Johnson, making no effort to conceal his anger. "You're suggesting we created this? That this school—*my* school—bred a *murderer*?"

Robertson tapped his foot against Johnson's under the desk. "Look, Mr. President, we aren't here to make accusations against the administration. That's not our intent. Maybe everyone missed the warning signs. It happens to all of us... But we do need your help before we miss any more."

"If I start handing over student records, letting you tear through private meetings... what happens to this institution?"

Robertson responded in a measured tone, "I understand. But try to see it this way. We are at a vital crossroads. Do you want to protect your students? Or let one get away with murder?"

Brightson looked hard into Robertson's eyes.

"Protect students? If you people aren't careful, there'll be no students left to protect."

"President Brightson—"

"You think this is about covering tracks? You have no idea what's about to happen here."

"Enlighten me," Robertson said.

"The moment this goes public, this campus becomes a battlefield. You'll have the media, the donors, the alumni—everyone taking sides. PIP has supporters, Inspector. So did Mr. Markowitz. This isn't just a murder case. It's a war over what this school stands for."

"Right now, it stands for a murder investigation," Johnson said. "And in the world of law enforcement, that, and the safety of the students, take precedence."

Brightson ignored Johnson and looked at Robertson. "Have you discussed this with Professor Kassimali, Inspector?"

Robertson and Johnson exchanged quick glances.

"Well, interesting you should ask," Robertson said.

"How so?"

"He declined to cooperate."

"Well, can't say that I blame him, given your wild theories."

"He's a person of interest in the investigation . . . and the police told him so."

Brightson clenched his jaw and glowered at Robertson.

"He's been feeding the fire of radicalism that consumed Ghazi. He may be involved," said Johnson.

Brightson leaned forward, his attention solely on Robertson. His expression darkened as he said loudly, "Professor Kassimali is one of this university's most prominent scholars. And more than that, he's critical to our survival. Do you have any idea how fragile funding for higher education is right now? Kassimali has brought in millions in donor support—millions that have kept this institution running. If you start dragging his name through the mud based on some fantasy-fueled theories, you won't just be disrupting one professor's career. You'll be jeopardizing the entire university. Be careful, Inspector. Be very, very careful."

Robertson rubbed his jaw and leaned in gently. "I understand—we know all about Kassimali's fundraising. But please realize that we're not the only ones watching it. That 'donor support' you're talking about? Some of it traces to offshore accounts with ties to extremist networks. And the money in those accounts? It's not just going toward scholarships or research grants. It supports terrorism... directly. We are only starting to unpeel that onion."

Brightson furrowed his brow and opened his mouth to speak.

Robertson beat him to it. "We're looking at a possible financial pipeline designed to systematically eliminate pro-Israel voices from this campus and beyond—through any means necessary. The protests, the intimidation, the smear campaigns—there's a pattern, and Kassimali's at the center of it."

"And now, a murder," added Johnson.

Brightson's fingers tightened around the edge of his desk. He continued to ignore Johnson. "That's an outrageous accusation. If you have evidence implicating Professor Kassimali, show it."

"We're inching there. There's some indication that Kassimali didn't just know about Ghazi's intent—he may have helped him plan it. It may be coincidental, I grant you, but Ghazi was seen leaving Kassimali's office several times.

There's also a digital trail we're following. If we find what we think we will, this goes beyond incitement. It becomes conspiracy to murder."

Brightson swiveled his chair to the left, turning once more to the window, through which the campus loomed. He let out a slow, measured breath and shook his head. Then, with a sharp inhale, he straightened his back, his expression hardening. "The university will cooperate with any further investigation. But I won't let you drag us through a political firestorm without undeniable proof. You are walking a dangerous line here."

"Understood. If Kassimali's hands are as clean as you think, you've got nothing to worry about. On the other hand, if the evidence is there... well, you know the answer." Robertson rose. "Many thanks for your time this morning."

He yanked his head at Johnson, who took the cue and rose. Brightson remained seated, saying nothing as his two guests left.

Outside the building, Robertson stopped. "Well, I guess I won't see you now... at least for a while."

Johnson shrugged.

"Where you headed?" Robertson said.

Johnson raised his hand goodbye and disappeared into the shadows.

21

A CALL TO PURPOSE

The conference room crackled with a charged intensity as revelations hung in the air. Voices rose and intertwined. Eyes widened. Hands carved meaning into the air. Heads tilted back in laughter, then forward in hushed reverence. A mosaic of expressive movements unfolded as the members of the CCJ delved deep within the labyrinth of their astonishing parallel histories, grappling with the dazzling weight of their past lives.

Melissa clutched her chest and exhaled sharply before clapping both hands over her mouth.

Across from her, Joshua leaned forward, elbows braced on the table, shaking his head slowly—once, twice—before letting out a stunned, breathy laugh. His gaze drifted to the ceiling, as if he were searching for something solid in the stark fluorescent light.

To his left, William rocked in his chair, rubbing the back of his neck, his mouth shaping a silent *wow*.

Beside him, Mary Jean, eyes glistening, placed a trembling hand on William's arm. She nodded, her expression hovering between awe and something even deeper, unnameable.

Michael flattened his palms against the table and leaned in, his shoulders rising with a shudder, and then broke into a grin, shaking his head at his own disbelief.

At opposite ends of the table, Caitlyn and Ash sat in silence, observing their young charges and exchanging satisfied, proud smiles. They had been here before—the rush of fragmented memories, the shock, the inevitable surrender to truth, all combusting into a staggering exhilaration.

Then a sharp, authoritative knock on the door broke the ambiance. The occupants of the room froze. Conversations severed mid-breath. Melissa's hand, still lifted as if sculpting an invisible thought, hesitated before dropping to the table. Michael, who had been laughing, head thrown back, snapped upright, his smile collapsing into a somber look.

The door swung open, and in the doorway stood a familiar, imposing figure.

Ash rose and addressed the visitor. "Good morning, President Brightson."

"Good morning, Professor Connor"—and with an acknowledging nod to the others around the table—"students, Professor Morrys."

In a jagged chorus, voices overlapping and out of sync, they responded, "Good morning, President Brightson."

Brightson scanned the room, his eyes searching. "Pardon the interruption. I was expecting to find Stephen Johnson here. He is part of this group, is he not?"

Ash responded, "Yes, yes, he is. And, in fact, we were wondering about him as well. He was supposed to be here, but he's been out of touch. No one seems to know where he is. It's like he's disappeared, gone on holiday or something."

Still leaning against the doorjamb, Brightson nodded. "I see." His gaze continued to roam around the room.

"Yeah, we're quite eager to ask him some questions," Melissa said.

Ash snapped his head toward her, giving her a sharp, disapproving look.

"I see. And why is that?" Brightson narrowed his eyes, his gaze drilling into her with evident keen interest.

Ash raised his hand in Melissa's direction, like a traffic cop, without looking at her. "Oh, nothing major. Just committee stuff. Passionate, thoughtful student."

Brightson nodded. "Well, as I said, sorry for the interruption. Enjoy your meeting."

He turned to leave and then stopped and turned back. "Of course, if you do run into him, please let him know I was hoping to get a few minutes of his time."

Ash nodded toward Brightson, who turned again and left, gently pulling the door shut behind him.

Everyone looked around at each other with inquiring eyes.

Mary Jean broke the ice. "Professor Connor, what happened to Stephen? I mean, he still has classes to attend, right?"

"Let's not worry about that," Ash said. "I'm sure he's fine. More importantly, we've got work to do. You five asked for a meeting. So let's meet. Melissa?"

"Thanks. I've been over this countless times. I still can't get my head around it. The memories feel so... raw. Hiding in basements, whispering in code, knowing one wrong word could mean a bullet to the head. It's a bit too much." She shook her head in disbelief.

"Exactly," Joshua said, leaning forward. "And that's why we can't just sit around and *talk* about this. We know what's coming—different names, different faces, but the same sickness, the same evil, the same campaign to wipe out the Jews. Extremism doesn't die. It mutates. And we, of all people, should know better than to do nothing but watch it spread."

"I hear you, Joshua," William said, folding his arms. "But let's not pretend action is simple. We fought from the shadows back then because there was no other choice. But now? Now we have influence, laws, social media, technology. Maybe our battle isn't about sabotage and resistance—maybe it's about education. Raising consciousness. Basic dialogue."

"You sound so calm, William. So detached," Melissa chimed in. "I mean, don't you feel the weight of it? Each day since we were at Robertson's house, I've awoken sweating, hearing their boots. Smelling the damp of those safe houses. I feel like... like I'm being *called* to do something. But then, I don't know. Some days, I just want to *forget*... and get my old life back. I want to be a student again, sit in a classroom, write papers, debate ideas."

"I understand what you're saying, Melissa," Joshua interposed. "I get it. But forgetting is what got us here. People forget, and history repeats. You saw what we did in those lives—we didn't hesitate. We risked everything because we knew it was the only way to stop the tide. Well, the tide is rising again. And I refuse to just watch. Nor should you."

A gentle voice interceded. "Joshua, I understand why you feel that way," said Mary Jean. "But disruption or violence—even in response to violence—only feeds the cycle. We can't let our past selves dictate how we respond now. We live in a different world. One where change happens in boardrooms, in classrooms, in communities, not just in dark alleys, with hushed plans. We need to be better. We need to set the bar high."

"I couldn't agree more," said Michael. "Look at history. The movements that lasted—that *worked*—they didn't meet hate with more hate. Civil rights, Gandhi, Mandela—real resistance is about standing firm, not striking first. And more than that, it perpetuates the value system we want. If we go the other way, we become them. Our souls will not evolve. We'll regress, and one thing we cannot afford to do is regress."

Joshua stood and went to grab a coffee refill. The room grew quiet. From several feet away, while pouring the hot liquid into his cup, he said, "What if standing firm isn't enough? What if words fail, like they did before?"

"Then we find another way," William said. "Not every battle is won with force. If we push too hard, we'll become just another faction. Another voice shouting into the storm."

"Yeah," Melissa said softly, "but if we don't push at all, we'll be droning on while the world burns."

Joshua turned to Caitlyn with pleading eyes, silently urging her to speak. She tipped her head upward, indicating they should continue their dialogue without her.

Mary Jean picked up the cue. "Pushing and fighting aren't the same thing. We *do* need to push—but through awareness, through policy, through human connection. Not through fear or aggression."

"Think about it—we're not just people with opinions," said Michael. "We remember. We've *been* here before. What if that's our gift? What if we can warn people, help them see the signs before it's too late?"

A brief silence fell.

Ash scanned the room, a knowing smile playing on his lips. He cleared his throat, the unmistakable signal that he was about to assume control of the discussion. "Look, here's my two cents. What you have undertaken is no small feat. To open your mind to the echoes of past lives, to submit to the unknown with courage, rather than fear—this is a testament to your character, your resilience, your curiosity, and your hunger for truth. Each of you has stepped beyond the veil of mere intellectualism into the vast, mysterious continuum of human experience. That alone is worthy of honor.

"You are now part of a lineage greater than yourselves, bound not only by blood but by soulful connection. But here's the thing, my young friends. That timeless connection comes with an obligation—to carry forward what you have learned in service of something greater. You did not walk through the corridors of time to emerge unchanged. Quite the contrary. You returned not just as scholars, but as stewards of the wisdom you have gained.

"The glimpses you caught—of other selves, other places, other stories—are not meant to be locked away, like ancient artifacts in a museum. They are maps, tools, and, perhaps most importantly, responsibilities. Let your past illuminate your present. Let it sharpen your sense of purpose.

"Now, the real work begins. What will you do with this knowledge? Will you use it to deepen your empathy, to better understand the struggles and triumphs of others? Will you apply it to your art, your science, your pursuit of justice? Will it help you mend wounds—your own and those of the world? History is not merely written in books. It is written in us. And we, in turn, have the power to shape the unwritten pages. You cannot—you must not—stand idle."

Melissa raised her hand meekly to shoulder height, and Ash nodded at her.

"Professor Connor, we hear your call. And you're right—knowledge is not an end. But what if we've learned but a fragment? What if we're not meant to go further at this point? What if we're not ready? Don't we have so much more to learn before we venture out?

"Yes, as you say, we've seen the echoes of the past, but the future still eludes us. Some of us were leaders once—warriors, visionaries—but are we meant to lead now? Or is our task to prepare the way for someone else—someone greater? I've felt it since our last session. A presence just beyond reach, as if history is bending toward a moment that has not yet arrived. What if the true guide, the one with the power and clarity to change everything, has not yet appeared to us? What if our purpose is not to lead, but to recognize that force when it comes—to stand ready and follow?"

Caitlyn smiled, a faint blush blooming on her cheeks, and leaned back in her chair. As if pulled by an unseen force, every gaze in the room settled on her as she said, "You did not step into those past lives by accident. You did not see what you saw merely to retreat into comfortable obscurity. And I will not let you sit idle while history calls your name.

"You are Jewish—each of you. That means something. It always has. Across centuries, across lifetimes, our people have carried the weight of survival, of wisdom, of leadership. And now, in this time—this fragile, trembling moment in history—that burden remains. Do you think it's coincidence that you, with your glimpses into the past, have been drawn together? No. It's a summons. There is no other interpretation."

Caitlyn spread her hands wide, as if issuing a challenge. "Israel stands on the edge of peril and possibility. Those murdered in Israel during the October 7 attack, who suffered at the hands of Hamas, cry out for justice and resolution. The world doesn't need another generation that turns its face away, that shrugs its shoulders and says, 'Not me. Not my task.' If not you, who? If not now, when? It's too convenient to put off until tomorrow what duty commands be done today.

"You saw your past lives? Good. Then you've seen the cycles of conflict, of exile, of power gained and lost. But history is not a prison—it is a teacher. If you have truly learned from it, then you will not accept the old failures. You will not be content with a world where your people live in fear and your neighbors live in despair.

"You were not shown the past so you could retreat into yourselves. That was no joy ride. You were shown the past so you could lead the way to something better. You owe this—not just to yourselves, not just to your ancestors, but to the future, which eagerly awaits your initiative. So I say: Rise to the moment. Be worthy of what you have seen. The world cannot afford your hesitation.

"I know this task feels immense. I know it feels beyond you. But hear me when I tell you—help is on the way, just as Melissa intimates.

"A new energy is rising, something—*someone*—who will bring a clarity we have not yet possessed. The world is shifting, and soon, there will be a force unlike any we have known. A presence that will guide, inspire, and illuminate the path forward.

"I cannot say more. Not yet. But I *feel* it, just as you have felt the echoes of your past lives. This is not the end of our journey—it is only the beginning. And I promise you, when the moment comes, you will understand.

"So do not falter now. Do not shrink back. The weight you carry is heavy, but it will not be yours alone for long.

"The one who is to come will show the way."

22

(RE)BIRTH

Ash skipped his usual early morning rendezvous with Caitlyn in the kitchen and set out for a solitary walk around the neighborhood. His body buzzed with anxiety, a jittery mix of worry and excitement, as if electric currents were tickling his insides. He sensed it in his bones—something thrilling was imminent. The anticipation left him dizzy.

He envisioned the grand hall of Windsor Castle, the staff bustling about with frantic energy, the air filled with the scent of freshly polished wood and the lingering sweetness of beeswax candles, their flames dancing against the backdrop of opulent tapestries. He muttered, "She is coming, she is coming," as he imagined himself eagerly awaiting the arrival of the Queen of England. The absurdity of the image made him laugh, a sound of self-mockery. His thoughts swung wildly back and forth—from trivial concerns, like whether the crib was too small, to existential musings about whether the world was too confined and ill-prepared for what was about to occur.

He plopped down on a park bench and ran a hand through his hair, taking it all in, then leaned back and drew in a deep breath. A conventional father would prepare for his child with cribs, blankets, and lullabies. But here he was, grappling with the magnitude of his daughter's impending birth. He had come to grips with the reality of past lives and accepted and embraced his genealogy. He had discovered himself, finally—no small feat for a man who, just a few months ago, had thought he had it all figured out, only to find out that his head had been jammed well below the sand for lo, these many years. An ache pressed against his ribs, as though something immense stirred within him, and his inner voice repeated, *She is coming, she is coming.*

And who was truly arriving? Not just the daughter he and Caitlyn had dreamed of—no, that would be far too ordinary. This was something greater, an arrival laden with destiny. He sensed it, as if he were witnessing the Red Sea parting before him—an emancipation from an old tyranny, a soulful awakening that seeped into his entire being like an unspoken but undeniable prophecy: *When your daughter opens her eyes, the world will tilt on its axis. Her first cry will cause the very air to shudder, heralding the rebirth of something ancient and profound.*

He thought, *I should be shaking with fear.* Perhaps it was hubris—Lord knew he had that in abundance—or perhaps he had succumbed to the hyperbole of Robertson and his wife and gotten caught up in spinning myths around the fragile, unformed body of an unborn child. And yet, he knew—knew it as surely as he felt his own breath, as naturally as he observed the sun rising and setting. Beneath his skin there resonated a quiet, unwavering certainty, much like the radiant glow of an expectant mother whose presence makes even strangers pause to sense the stirrings beneath her belly. One day, the world would call her, and when that happened,

(Re)birth

he—and Caitlyn—would have to let her go. The weight of this truth was nearly unbearable. Yet he would bear it without hesitation, for it was not his burden alone. She would forever be theirs to love, guide, and protect, for as long as fate allowed. Wouldn't she?

A sudden gust struck him squarely in the face, shattering his composure and sending a shiver cascading up his spine. It was time to return to his wife—time for the miracle of birth to unfold and shock the world.

By the time Ash entered the house, Caitlyn had already moved into the reconfigured bedroom. He laughed to himself, acknowledging that while they were a pretty good team, no way would Caitlyn stand on ceremony for something like this. When the time came, she would be all business. He rushed up the stairs to join the assembled group.

The two of them had planned diligently for this moment, preparing not merely for a birth but for a sacred, waterborne arrival of deep significance. They'd had countless in-depth discussions with their midwife and health-care team to ensure every concern was addressed, every possibility explored. They'd carefully reviewed the birth plan, deliberated over contingencies, pored over each decision with the utmost care—everything was to be executed with the precision of an elite military unit on a critical mission. But it had not been just a series of tasks—it was a labor of love, a dedication to certifying that every aspect of the experience would honor the arrival of their baby. It was the miracle of new life, after all, that they were about to witness.

In the quiet of their chosen birthing room, they prepared the pool. Ash had selected a spacious tub, ensuring that Caitlyn could move freely while the warm water gently cradled the baby. The midwife had scrubbed and disinfected all surfaces, erasing any trace of worry with each swipe of the medical-grade cleaner. She'd strategically placed the pillows, towels, and familiar comfort items, each a small token of love. Safety was paramount—vital equipment and emergency supplies lay within easy reach, a silent promise that they'd taken every precaution. The team—a dedicated midwife, a compassionate nurse, and a reassuring obstetrician—moved with synchronized precision, each person aware of their role in this life-changing event.

In their final moments of quiet reflection, Caitlyn practiced taking deep, calming breaths while Ash gently held her hand, both savoring the anticipation of what was to come. They shared a glance, a mutual understanding that the world around them was about to shift in ways they had only dared to imagine.

The scent of lavender lingered in the air, mingled with the faint tang of warm water and the earthy undertones of sage smoldering in a small clay dish. At the center of the space, the birth pool—round, deep, and encircled by a soft, inflatable rim—sat like a placid, waiting basin.

As the pool filled, the water was heated to between 36°C and 37°C—that perfect, womb-like temperature—and monitored carefully to provide an oasis of comfort. The windows, cracked just slightly, allowed the fresh morning air to slip through, cool and crisp, rustling the sheer white curtains, which billowed like ghostly prayers. Soft lighting infused the room, transforming the space into a serene haven.

The midwife stood close to Caitlyn, her presence steady but unobtrusive, her hands warmed by experience, her gaze keen and watchful. Around her neck, a simple string of wooden beads rested against her linen dress, her fingers stroking them instinctively as she listened to the rhythm of Caitlyn's breath, the way the water moved with her contractions.

Everything stood poised in silent expectation—the water, the light, even the air itself, as if holding its breath, awaiting the moment when the stillness would shatter and a new voice would awaken the world.

Downstairs, the members of the CCJ gathered in quiet anticipation—everyone except Stephen Johnson, who remained incommunicado. Caitlyn had asked Joshua to recite a prayer, and while the others took their seats, he paced nervously downstairs, waiting for Ash's signal. The student group sat in thoughtful silence until a single voice broke through the stillness.

"Joshua!"

Startled, Joshua leaped to his feet as if jolted by lightning. Glancing back, he caught sight of his colleagues, who were offering him encouraging thumbs-ups and warm smiles. With newfound energy, he bounded up the stairs to join Ash.

"Let's go, son," Ash said gently.

Joshua pulled a folded piece of paper from his pocket, shuffled into the room, and approached the side of the tub. After receiving a nod from Ash, he announced, "The Sacred Waters: A Birth Psalm." As Caitlyn offered a thin, knowing smile and closed her eyes, Joshua began to recite the prayer with quiet conviction.

> Hear, O soul, the whisper of the deep,
> A voice that stirs where waters sleep.
> The breath of dawn, the pulse of light,
> The Lord is One—pure, infinite.

> Blessed be the Name that ever flows,
> In silent stars, in tides that know.
> From first-born breath to final sigh,
> His love is written on the sky.
>
> Bind this truth upon your chest,
> A seal of peace, a whispered rest.
> Let waters hold you, soft and bright,
> Like rivers drawn to holy light.
>
> The world is waiting, still and wide,
> A child emerges, eyes open, wise.
> A voice unspoken fills the air,
> The Lord is here. The Lord is there.

The water shimmered in the tub, rippling with each contraction. Caitlyn gasped, her body straining against the force of something greater than herself. The air inside the room thickened—not just with the scent of lavender and sage, but with something ancient, something electric. Ash knelt at the edge of the birthing pool, his hands hovering above the water, his fingers trembling as if caught in a hidden current.

"This is it," he whispered. "The return."

Caitlyn arched, her moans becoming deeper, primal, sounding less like pain and more like prophecy. Outside, the wind picked up, howling through the trees, but inside the room, everything stilled. The midwife, a middle-aged woman with blonde-streaked braids, watched with wide eyes.

Then the water darkened—not with blood, but with something richer. A golden radiance spread from beneath Caitlyn's belly—not a reflection of candlelight, but something intrinsic, something otherworldly. The room grew warmer, as if touched by an unseen sun.

Ash's breath hitched. "Do you see that?"

(Re)birth

The midwife nodded once but said nothing.

Then the wooden beams overhead groaned. A low, resounding creak, like old doors swinging open. The candle flames bent—not flickering but bowing, all at once—toward the birth pool, as if in reverence. The scent of the air changed subtly, impossibly—frankincense, pure and holy, curling through the room like a whisper from antiquity.

And then the child came.

Not in the usual tumbling, frenzied chaos of birth, but with tranquility. The baby slipped into the gold-stained water and did not thrash. Did not wail. The midwife reached down, hands steady, and lifted the child.

Ash and Caitlyn gasped.

The infant's eyes were open—wide.

Not the glassy, unfocused gaze of a newborn, but piercing and knowing, ancient and calm. A beautiful wisdom sat in their depths, the weight of lifetimes folded into the small form. The midwife turned the baby, allowing her to take her first breath.

Then a burst of wind tore through the house, rattling the wooden walls, sending the candles shuddering. Outside, the cumulus clouds parted to reveal a blindingly bright sun overhead.

Ash felt something inside him crack open. Like a door unlocking in the marrow of his bones, a knowledge pressing into his chest.

Then he looked out the window and saw a dove fluttering outside, hovering just beyond the window, its wings beating in slow, deliberate strokes, as if suspended between earth and sky. Its dark eyes peered inside, unblinking, serene—watching. A silent witness. A quiet blessing.

Ash turned to Caitlyn and said, his voice barely a whisper, "This is—"

The child blinked.

And in the hush of that sacred moment, the wind died. The water stilled. The candles righted themselves. The dove departed. Outside, the first raindrops touched the earth—though the sky remained clear.

Caitlyn cradled the child to her chest, tears slipping silently down her face. Ash knelt beside her, his hands pressed together, his heart hammering against his rib cage.

Something had begun.

* * *

The magical event had been shared as a group, but after everyone left, Ash and Caitlyn stole some private time.

"She hasn't even cried, you know," Ash said.

"No. She just... opened her eyes, looked at me as if we'd known each other for lifetimes. As if she was waiting for us to catch up to her." Caitlyn stroked the baby's smooth cheek.

"It's a little terrifying, don't you think?" He shook his head and exhaled slowly.

"What is?" Caitlyn glanced at her husband, furrowing her brow.

Ash leaned in, like he was going to share a secret, and then whispered, "That she's not just ours. That she never really was."

Caitlyn pulled the baby to her chest, wrapping both arms around her. "She's ours," she said, holding her more firmly. "She's our daughter first... and always will be. No matter what else she is... or becomes. She'll always be ours."

(Re)birth

"She's more, Caitlyn. We both felt it. We've always known it... or at least, of late it's become more and more apparent. I mean, the way the water moved around her before she ever appeared. I hadn't imagined that. The damn room *shifted* when she took her first breath."

Caitlyn tightened her grip on the baby and said nothing.

"You saw how the midwife looked. She knew. Even the air felt different. Still does."

Caitlyn kept her gaze fixed on the baby. When she finally spoke, it sounded like she was talking to herself. "The world will call to her."

"Yes," Ash said, nodding, his jaw tightening, "and one day we'll have to let her go."

Caitlyn started to cry softly and gripped the child even more tightly. "She's still just a baby. She still needs us... me." The last word came out in a softer, tearful voice.

"I know," Ash said, placing a hand on top of Caitlyn's arm and squeezing gently. "And we'll protect her as long as we can." He paused and took a deep breath. "But Caitlyn... she won't just grow up. She'll become something else, and I worry we won't be equipped to be parents in the normal sense. We may be in over our heads. Whatever happens, we may be powerless to stop it."

The room fell silent, the only sound the faint, steady rhythm of their daughter's breathing.

Then Caitlyn spoke quietly. "Our job, my sweet, is to make sure that, before the world gets to her, she knows who she is. That she's loved, that she's good, that she's essential... that no matter how far she moves beyond us, she will never be alone. We will always be there for her."

Ash leaned back and pulled his hand away from Caitlyn and the baby. He nodded several times to himself before speaking. "Then that's what we'll do. That's what we can do."

Caitlyn smiled and said, "Odd, I'm not even tired. I'm raring to go. How're you feeling?"

"I'm feeling that I'm no God denier, that's for sure," he said, his voice rising slightly.

Caitlyn smiled even wider. "I love you, Ash."

"I love you too."

Ash leaned in and kissed Caitlyn on the temple and then planted a gentle kiss on his daughter's tiny forehead. The baby shifted in response, a soft sigh escaping her tiny body, and for a few seconds, time bowed to them, honoring their fragile shared moment, before the world changed forever.

ACKNOWLEDGMENTS

First and foremost, I would like to acknowledge my life partner, best friend, and husband, Joseph Farber. The pandemic crisis that the world faced completely altered my life-cycle pattern. To accommodate a very hectic work schedule, which involved months of remote learning, instruction, and administration, I would rise at 2:30 in the morning, go to the gym, and then write this novel for several hours every day. I could not have ventured off into the world of creative writing without my husband, who has always been my greatest encourager and supporter. Our discussions around this particular manuscript, and the critiques and revisions that resulted, were greatly appreciated.

Next, my four sons: Jeremy, Jonathan, Douglas, and, of course, Andrew. My experiences with you—all of you—have taught me to be a parent and teacher. I am so grateful to you for the love and acceptance you have given me over the years. When I look at the four of you, I am truly amazed by who you are and what you have become. I love and adore your wives—Daniella, Aviva, Christine, and Melissa—for who they are and how they have helped you create such extraordinary families. I am also blessed to have wonderful grandchildren who have given me and Joseph the greatest joy in life. To all of you—Olivia, Zachary, Noa, Lincoln, Lilybelle, Quinn, Harrison, and Lily—I now wait with great expectation to see how each of you will turn out. I know I will enjoy watching you grow up with your parents—my children. The cycle of life is an extraordinary circle, and I believe in my heart that we are all souls that have traveled through time together.

Finally, I would like to thank and acknowledge my extraordinary editor, Michael Coffino. You have been my advisor and chief critic through the multiple drafts of both of my books. I will always be grateful for your belief in me and these projects.

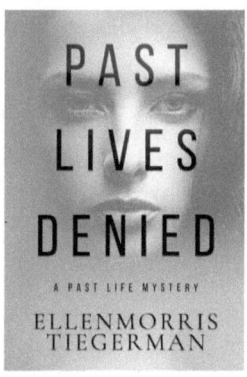

How deep would you go to find the truth?

Glamorous and eccentric, Caitlyn Morrys isn't like the other professors at her small Midwestern college. But her real eccentricity isn't just her meticulous style and outspoken nature—Caitlyn has always believed she's had past lives.

Or are her persistent flashbacks of other times and places merely dreams?

When a political storm breaks out over teacher tenure and academic freedom on campus, Caitlyn never expects to be at the center of it. Then the school's president, her bitter adversary, is found brutally killed in his office.

Acting chief inspector Cormac Robertson, a staunch proponent of past-life regression, is convinced that the only way to solve the murder is through excavation of Caitlyn's past lives via hypnotism. When under his spell, Caitlyn reveals more than she ever realized she knew.

But the killer's vengeance for a past-life betrayal is unfinished...

And Caitlyn's ability puts a target on her back.

Revenge, betrayal, and spiritual experiences collide in this thrilling mystery exploring past-life regression, the first book in the Past Lives Mysteries Trilogy.

ABOUT THE AUTHOR

Dr. Ellenmorris Tiegerman is the Executive Director of Tiegerman School and a Professor Emeritus at the Derner Institute for Advanced Psychology Studies at Adelphi University. As the founder of Tiegerman School, Dr. Tiegerman is responsible for the creation and the development of the preschool, school age, and integrated programs within the school.

In 1994, Dr. Tiegerman served on Governor Pataki's Transition Team for Education. She was appointed in 1995 by means of an Assembly appointment to the 21st Century Schools Committee. In 1996, Dr. Tiegerman was appointed by means of a gubernatorial recommendation to the New York State Early Intervention Coordinating Council. Most recently, Dr. Tiegerman served as Chairperson of the Parent Involvement Committee.

Dr. Tiegerman has served on the faculty of several universities in the New York Metropolitan area. She has functioned as the Director of the Adelphi University Speech and Hearing Center as well as being the Founding Director of the Adelphi University Preschool Language Stimulation Program.

Dr. Tiegerman holds a PhD from the City University of New York. She also has Masters degrees in: Speech Language Pathology (MS and MPhil), Special Education (MS) and Social Work (MSW). She has extensive experience in the areas of child language development and disorders. She has been involved in many research projects and is the author of textbooks in the areas of language disorders, early intervention, parent language training, and childhood autism. Dr. Tiegerman's area of clinical expertise is autism spectrum disorders.

www.ingramcontent.com/pod-product-compliance
Lightning Source LLC
LaVergne TN
LVHW041916070526
838199LV00051BA/2639